DARK CORNERS

by Michael Arruda

Trevor waited, as if to make sure Dee understood. Then he gently placed the roach on her lips.

It quickly scurried from her mouth up the side of her nose towards her forehead. Just as fast, Dee grabbed the insect, pulling it off her face. Trevor's expression went sour. His face filled with anxiety, as if he feared she were about to ruin the moment, but she didn't toss the bug onto the floor. Instead, she calmly lowered it to just above her lips. She opened her mouth wide and dropped the roach inside.

She closed her mouth and chewed, slowly, methodically, as if she were savoring each and every bite, as if nothing she had ever eaten had tasted this good. The reality was far from it. The roach tasted horribly bitter, like blood mixed with dirt. She tried to make things better by imagining she was eating sunflower seeds. After several seconds, the taste of blood in her mouth became less nauseating, and she didn't have to pretend any longer that she was enjoying the experience. The coppery taste grew on her, as she rolled around the bits and pieces now mixed with her saliva inside her mouth, touching each morsel with her tongue, pausing to play with it against her teeth.

"Mmm," she moaned slowly.

Trevor trembled ever so slightly, and he wiped drool from his lips.

Slowly, she swallowed.

"Mmm," she moaned again. "That was good."

She suddenly felt exposed, as if she were lying naked in front of him.

He smiled at her gently and said, "It's okay. I won't tell."

First edition

For lovers of the dark
And
Those who live by the light
In constant conflict
Together they form shadows
From which
Emerge
Dark Corners

"There is evil in this world. There are dark awful things. Occasionally we get a glimpse of them. But there are *dark* corners; horrors almost impossible to imagine—even in our worst nightmares. There is a Satan."

—Peter Cushing as Professor Van Helsing in DRACULA A.D. 1972 (1972)

Contents

"Dark Corners" was originally published in 2001 in the anthology *New Traditions in Terror*, edited by Bill Purcell. The impetus for this story was its setting: I once lived in an apartment building in Boston which featured a creepy old elevator like the one in this story. Like I do with many experiences in my life, I pocketed this elevator until the right story came along, and that story was "Dark Corners."

DARK CORNERS

She pressed the button, and following several silent minutes, her client responded without saying a word, buzzing her into the large Boston apartment building.

She stepped into the low-lit lobby, her briefcase in hand, and made for the elevator. "Out of Order" the sign read.

Ann looked to her right. The base of a winding staircase.

"Sullivan's on the sixth floor," she muttered. "Should have packed the sneakers."

As she climbed the first set of stairs which wrapped around the elevator shaft—it was one of those old-fashioned elevators, the ones with the caged doors and the screened enclosures, which meant she could see directly into the shaft: the broken down elevator appeared to be parked on the basement bottom— she suddenly found herself in darkness. Whereas the lobby had boasted a poor excuse of a chandelier which would have struggled to light a small closet, never mind a tall hallway, here there was nothing. No ceiling lights, no lamps on the wall, nothing.

The darkness unnerved Ann, and she gripped her briefcase tightly. There was a can of Mace inside, which she carried whenever she had business inside the city. She wasn't paranoid. She was a realist. She knew the stats, the number of women raped each day. She had no intention of becoming a statistic. She wondered if she should remove the can, hold it in her hand.

As she ascended the steps towards the second floor, she began to perspire. Not from exhaustion, which would have been embarrassing for someone who went to aerobics three times a week, but from fear. She *could not see,* and suddenly she was more afraid of being injured than getting attacked.

"What the hell is Thomas Sullivan doing living in a place like this?" she asked herself.

Thomas Sullivan, her client, was a wealthy Boston businessman, long retired, and dying, which was why he couldn't visit her at the office, and why she was there now making a house call, to revise his will. She had never met the man, but as his estate planning attorney, she felt she knew an awful lot about him, especially after having immersed herself in his finances the last couple of weeks. He was rich and should have been living in one of the finest apartment buildings Boston had to offer. At the very least, a place that could afford to pay its electric bills!

As she felt her way past the second floor, the distinct odor of urine filled the staircase.

Her pace quickened, her heels clomping loudly on the hard marble steps.

She was grateful her route around the elevator remained the same. Ten straight steps ascending upwards towards a wider set which curved around the rear of the elevator shaft, leading to a new group of twenty straight steps that advanced to the next floor. There, a flat hallway jutted out to the left in front of the broken elevator. This brief hall, about ten paces, led to the next level of stairs.

She had reached the fifth floor when the smell of urine became mixed with the more pleasant aroma of fabric softener. She could also smell the faint scent of pipe tobacco.

As she prepared to ascend the last set of stairs, the ones which would finally take her to her destination, the sixth floor, she stopped.

There was something strange about the darkened corner above her. She was surrounded by darkness, engulfed by it, but ahead of her was something even darker. It reminded her of the nights she had driven the rural interstates of New Hampshire, her home state, and come upon a storm. Driving in complete darkness with only her headlights as guides, she'd look up to see the stars gone, and in their place something darker than dark, an ominous black blur, a storm cloud, hovering there above her like the Titanic, waiting to ingest her and everything around her into its void. She'd shiver and pray to God she'd get home safely.

Darker than dark.

She froze, unable to take another step.

Perhaps there was something there, an object, a large misplaced dresser, for instance, discarded in the hall by some tired mover, exhausted from carrying furniture up and down the winding staircase. Since she still held her briefcase in her right hand, she raised her left in front of her, to protect herself lest she bump into the expected object which she could not see.

Cautiously, she advanced to the next step.

A pale face, as white as chalk, emerged from the dark corner, and Ann sucked in a gasp which nearly imploded her tonsils.

The face was that of an old man, a man with a high forehead, a crooked nose that looked as jagged as an iceberg, and a small unassuming mouth. His eyes were on fire, flaming red, burning in direct contrast to the pale lifeless ash which served as his skin. No eyebrows, eyelashes, or facial hair of any kind adorned his face, and he was as bald as a newborn and just as discolored.

He stepped from the corner, his sheet white hands nearly glowing in the dark, his fingers outstretched and long, like serpents arched to strike.

Ann tried to scream, but in one quick sweeping motion the old man advanced from the corner, grabbed her by the throat, impeding any sound which might have resonated from her vocal chords, and whirled her around.

His bony fingers were as cold as ice, and with them wrapped around her throat, he lifted her clear off her feet, her high-heeled shoes slipping to the floor, her hosed toes wriggling, dangling above the step. She dropped her briefcase as she grabbed onto his hands with both of hers in an unsuccessful attempt to tear them away from her throat. He forced her into the corner, smacking the back of her head against the wall. Seeing that she was losing consciousness, the old man removed his pressing fingers from her windpipe, allowing her to suck in deep breaths of air.

He now held her by the sides of her neck, and using both his hands, tilted her head, exposing the left side of her throat completely. She watched as his tongue protruded from his mouth and licked his lips with anticipation. She wanted to scream, but she couldn't muster enough breath to make even a whimper.

He opened his mouth, reared back his lips, and exposed an exaggerated pair of incisors. With his tongue, he licked their tips. She cringed, and he zeroed in for the jugular.

A loud bang from the floor below jolted the both of them.

Light!

A door on the fifth floor had slammed open, firing waves of light into every crevice of the darkened stairwell, but falling inches shy of Ann and her attacker, who remained partially hidden in the shadows.

The old man wanted to nudge Ann further into the corner, but at so close a proximity to the opened door, he dared not move. For the moment, both his eyes and Ann's were riveted to the floor below.

A young woman, not a day over twenty-one, with large firm breasts which stood erect in her tight sweater, marched angrily into the stairwell. A man leapt out after her.

"Vicki, please!"

"Please, *what!*"

"Don't go. Hear me out."

Simultaneously, the old man and Ann turned their eyes towards each other. The pale attacker gently placed Ann's feet to the floor, and raising the long bony index finger of his right hand to his lips, whispered, "Shh!"

Ann thought, "You've got to be kidding!"

He read her expression and motioned with the same index

finger, slicing it across his neck menacingly, warning her of the consequences should she disobey his wishes.

"I told you, *no!*" Vicki wailed from the bright doorway. "And here's your stupid ring back! It's not even a real diamond, you loser!"

She thrust the ring to the floor, as he muttered a barely audible, "It's all I could afford!"

It was the last thing on her mind at the moment, considering her own predicament, but Ann had never witnessed or even imagined for that matter a breakup as horrendously painful as the one occurring on the floor below them.

As the woman stomped angrily down the stairs leading to the fourth floor, Ann realized that the argument was all but over which meant her assailant would pick up where he left off. She quickly considered her options. The can of Mace lay in her briefcase, which had fallen to the wide step just below their feet. So close, yet she didn't see how she could reach it. This man holding onto her looked as if he might die at any moment, but he was as strong and as solid as her aerobic instructor. More so. Try as she might, she could not break his grip from her.

That left only one other option.

Scream!

In the same millisecond that her mouth opened, the old man looked down upon her with disappointment. He lifted his right hand, shaking his index finger back and forth like a disapproving nun scolding her Catholic school children. This same right hand then catapulted towards her throat, grasping her windpipe, blocking both air and sound from passing through.

"Here's some advice, Eric," Vicki shouted from the staircase below, "the next time you propose to someone, keep your pants on!"

"It was a joke!"

"Yeah, it was a joke!"

"Vicki! Come back! *Please!*

"Please come back." He was sobbing now. He stood there a moment, with both the old man and a stifled Ann watching him from the dark corner above. When it became apparent

Vicki wasn't coming back, Eric turned around and reentered the hallway, slamming the door shut behind him.

Darkness reigned once more.

The old man smiled. He had been looking over his shoulder to see the proceedings downstairs, and as he turned his head back towards Ann, he saw that his intended victim had turned purple.

He quickly released his grip on her windpipe, and this time as she gasped for air, he allowed her to drop to her knees. She remained there a moment, sucking in huge breaths of air, giant gulps of life.

The old man remained above her, patiently waiting for her to catch her breath.

The sharp sound of breaking glass, and the old man reflexively turned away, looking down towards the fifth floor, from where the sound had apparently come.

Ann looked up and saw her assailant distracted. She was on her hands and knees, and her right hand was inches from her briefcase. This was her best chance. She reached inside and thanked God almighty that on her first try her fingers found the can of Mace. She ripped it out and shot it up towards the old man's face, the face that was looking directly down at her.

With the speed of a cat, he swiped the can from her hand—she cried out, in complete and utter disbelief at both the quickness with which he had moved and the strength he had displayed in tearing the Mace from her grasping fingers. She couldn't believe her weapon was now in his hands. It wasn't possible. And she hadn't seen anything yet. He closed his fingers around the can and *crushed* it, like it was made of Styrofoam.

She laughed a nervous insane laugh, and slouched down so that her bottom rested upon the steps. The old man stepped towards her.

Eric crashed down upon his kitchen floor, his butt hitting the grease-stained tiles hard. In his hand, a shard of glass the size of the Biggie drink he had sucked down earlier in the evening. He was sitting in the corner, his left shoulder pressed upon the stove and the heels of his sneakers touching the refrigerator. The kitchen was so small that he couldn't open the fridge and the oven at the same time, for their doors would collide.

He lifted both his arms. His right hand held the blade of glass, which hovered over his bare left wrist.

"Come on! Do it!" he exclaimed aloud.

He motioned with the glass, slicing at air, but he couldn't bring himself to follow through. He dropped the shard to the floor and began to sob uncontrollably.

"*I'm sick of my life!* Is there something wrong with me? — that no woman—Is there something wrong?" cried the twenty-three-year-old virgin. "Just once, God! How about giving me a break, just *once*?"

"If I were a real man I'd have a gun, so I could blow my brains out! But no, I don't believe in guns! I'm Mr. Sensitive! A lot of good that does me!"

Eric's head slouched to the side, bumping the oven.

His eyes widened.

On the staircase, the old man reached down and grasped Ann from underneath her armpits. In the gentlest of motions, he lifted her to her feet. He then straightened out her disheveled clothes, even taking the time to dust some of the floor dirt off her suit jacket.

Ever so gently, he nudged her backwards, deeper into the corner, until her back touched the wall.

She was in a stupor now, brought there initially by fear, and held there by a set of burning eyes that commanded her attention.

He placed his fingertips softly upon her right cheek and slowly turned her head to the left, exposing her bare neck completely. He smiled, placed his hands upon her shoulders, and lowered his mouth to within an inch of her throat, when he stopped to blow whispers of air onto her flesh, giving her goose bumps.

Eric shoved his head into the oven.

The old man's lips finally made contact, kissing the area around her jugular, licking it, moistening it, preparing it for what was next to come.

He raised his head again, away from her neck, and opened his mouth. His protruding incisors throbbed with desire.

He dove for her throat, his tongue lapping the combined flavors of skin, perfume, and sweat. There was only one flavor missing.

Blood.

He bit down and broke her flesh.

Just a small puncture, no larger than a pinpoint. The tiniest drops of blood oozed from the minuscule wounds, and he quickly but neatly lapped them up.

"Son of a bitch!" Eric exclaimed, angered that he was still alive. "What the hell's wrong with this oven? Why isn't it working?"

The old man's fangs reentered the wounds. It was time to rip her open-time to feast.

Eric lit a match.

There was a flash, which only Eric saw, although he would never remember it. To the rest of the apartment's occupants, there was only an explosion, a blast that rocked the entire building.

The old man was blown on top of Ann, pinning her against the wall, his fangs completely missing their mark, scraping against the mildew-covered plaster instead. As they bounced backwards, Ann fell to her knees, and the old man lost his balance, stumbling down the steps, smashing into the paper thin cage surrounding the open elevator shaft.

He fell through, taking the crumpled mess of rotting wire with him as he plummeted six stories down to the basement below, landing on top of the parked elevator with a loud thud and a spattering of dust.

It was raining, as it always seemed to do whenever Ann attended a funeral. As she and Kent climbed the glistening stone steps leading up to Hoyt's Funeral Home, her friend and colleague couldn't help but find humor in the situation.

"That guy sure as hell had shit for luck! All he wanted to do was kill himself. Instead, he blows up half his building, injures a dozen people, kills Tom Sullivan, and worst of all for him, *survives* the whole thing! Now he's being charged with reckless endangerment and manslaughter! He's looking at ten to twenty years. Poor bastard should have killed himself! All I can say is, thank God you hadn't reached Sullivan's apartment. You're a lucky woman!"

"Lucky," Ann repeated under her breath.

Kent, of course, was referring to her lack of injuries. She had been treated and released from the hospital the same day.

He didn't know about the attack. Nobody knew, because she had yet to mention it to anyone.

She had seen her attacker crash through the screen. Had heard him hit bottom. Had seen his dead body lying on top of the elevator. She knew he was dead because his neck appeared broken.

Yet, rescue workers recovered only one dead body at the scene: Tom Sullivan, and he was killed in his apartment.

She was confused and afraid.

She realized the longer she kept things to herself, the more difficulty she'd have getting people to believe her. Perhaps after the wake, she'd tell Kent. She knew she had to tell somebody. She *had* been attacked. She knew it. She just didn't want to be called crazy.

Kent escorted Ann into the funeral hall, where they checked their coats and moved on to offer their condolences to the family of Thomas Sullivan. Having done so, it was time to pay their respects in silent prayer over the body of the deceased.

"I hate open caskets," Kent whispered into Ann's ear, while they waited in line behind more than two dozen of Mr. Sullivan's family members and friends.

Ann hated them too, but that was the last thing bothering her at the moment. She knew what she had to tell Kent upon leaving the building, and it terrified her, made her feel vulnerable.

"Stop feeling this way," she told herself. "You're the victim, remember? You were attacked! You *were!* You didn't imagine it!"

When the time came for them to pay their respects, Kent led Ann to the kneeler in front of the open coffin, and the two attorneys knelt together in front of the body.

Ann blessed herself and started to pray as she looked upon Mr. Sullivan for the first time.

She nearly swallowed her tongue: the man in the coffin was

the man who had attacked her! Her body temperature raged to boiling hot proportions, and she fought to control herself.

"Don't lose it in front of all these people! Am I going crazy? Is this possible?"

She gazed intensely into the pale face, the bald hairless face. It was him.

He opened his eyes!

She gave a start, but he turned his eyes upon her, holding her still momentarily, and with a quick terse motion, raised his right hand to his mouth and uttered a soft, "Shh!"

Shaking uncontrollably, Ann pivoted to her left to see Kent's eyes closed in silent prayer, and then she passed out.

It was still raining, had been for three days, but that's not what had awoken her.

She was already awake. She was *waiting*.

She looked to the wide-open window of her Brookline apartment: the long white curtains were flowing madly in the warm summer night's breeze. The rain was coming in.

A moment before, the window had been open but a crack..

Her eyes roved to the far corner of her bedroom, and there recognized the frightening impenetrable darkness she had first encountered in that fateful corner of Sullivan's hallway. That same mountain of black was now hovering menacingly in her room.

Ann swallowed.

From her extreme right came the creaking of her favorite rocking chair. She looked in its direction.

Nothing but darkness.

And the repetitive clacking of wood on wood.

Then, as if lit internally, two white bony hands appeared resting on either side of the arms of the chair. Next, the face. Pale, hairless, and very much alive. He sat there, rocking, the only sound in the room the creaking of the chair against the hard-wood floor.

His face was full of desire, as if he were eager to obtain that which had nearly been his five nights before.

He stopped rocking.

Ann remained motionless under the covers, too terrified to move.

The vampire arose.

He approached the bed, nearly gliding across the floor, and he must have been dressed in black, for Ann still could see nothing of him other than his face and hands.

When he reached the side of the bed, he stood there a moment, looking down upon Ann, as if to admire his prize. He raised his right hand and gently stroked the left side of her face, his fingers like icicles upon her skin. He nudged her face to the side, once more exposing her throat.

He smiled, looking over his unfinished work, the two minuscule puncture wounds on her neck, directly above her jugular. He licked his incisors, and then bent down towards her throat.

Ann shot her right hand, which had been hidden underneath the bed clothes, upwards towards her attacker's own throat. In her hand, was a knife. She sliced a wound across the entire length of his neck, his undead flesh tearing easily.

He jumped backwards, grasping his throat, more from shock than from pain or fear.

Ann shoved the sheets from her body and leapt from the bed, landing on the opposite side from the vampire. In her right hand she still clasped the knife, and in her left, a crucifix, which she extended towards the vampire's face.

He scowled and looked away, momentarily, the crucifix providing him with a mere annoyance, like a light aimed at his eyes.

His hand was still on his neck, and although the wound ran nearly from ear to ear, there was no blood. He had not fed yet. His innards were dry.

When he next looked upon Ann, there was a different countenance about him. Gone was the polite old man who simply wanted to feed upon the blood of this luscious young woman. In his place was a vengeful monster, furious, outraged, betrayed, desiring to inflict as much pain upon his victim as possible.

He stepped towards her, and by the rapidity with which he

walked, his intentions were clear: he was going to rip the knife and crucifix from her hands and ravage her beautiful neck, draining her body of every last drop of its blood.

Ann retreated and bumped the wall, whimpering, knowing there was nowhere else to go.

Suddenly, the vampire stopped. He again reached for the wound on his throat when to his surprise felt *pain*.

He teetered, and then dropped to his knees.

It was Ann's turn to smile. "This knife, Mr. Sullivan, is made from pure *silver*, the one element that vampires abhor. In fact, its touch can be fatal."

The vampire opened its mouth, perhaps to utter some foul curse, but Ann raced her right hand to her face, and still holding the knife in her fist, extended her index finger to her lips.

"Shh!" she whispered.

The vampire rolled his eyes and collapsed face first onto the hardwood floor.

Dead.

Ann dropped her weapons and snagged her cordless phone. She hit the third speed dial key and waited for Kent to pick up.

"Kent? Sorry about the late hour. Listen, you'd better get over here to my apartment, and bring Brian Moses with you. I'm going to need a criminal attorney. I'll explain everything when you get here. And Kent? You'd better give the lawyer representing Eric Saunders a call. Tell him that his client's luck has just changed."

She looked down at the dead old man on the floor.

"I've just given the poor bastard something to live for."

"Untouchable" was the lead story in the anthology *Death Grip: Legacy of Terror*, edited by Walt Hicks and published in 2003. I wrote the story after reading a newspaper article on India's caste system.

UNTOUCHABLE

H-*h-hoot. Hoot.*
      Drip-drop. Drip-drop.
I am a Dalit.

A member of India's caste system.

Outlined in our ancient sacred text, the Rig Veda, our caste system divides people into four groups —the Brahmins, or priests, the Kshatriyas, or soldiers, the Vaisyas, or artisans, and the Sudras, the farmers and the peasants.

Beneath these four groups is a fifth group. The group to which I belong.

The Dalits.

We are excluded from the four main groups because we are not considered part of human society.

Higher caste Hindus will not even touch us. If they do, they perform rituals to cleanse themselves. Even our shadows mustn't fall on them.

We are the "untouchables."

There are 240 million Dalits living in India. That's nearly 25% of the population. One out of every four people in my country is an "untouchable."

My name is Dhara, and I'm sixteen-years old.

I live with my mother and little brother Mitesh in the shanty town of Trilokpuri, a slum of New Delhi. Nearly 10,000 people live here in Trilokpuri, an impoverished little wasteland on the far side of the Yamuna river. Horrible things have happened here. Things that defy description. Poverty drives people to act in bestial ways.

I'm no exception.

I never wanted anyone to die.

I just wanted to save my brother. What big sister wouldn't want that?

Little Mitesh.

He's ten, but he has the body of a five-year-old. The result of malnutrition and sickness.

Like most Dalits in Trilokpuri, we don't have access to health care. Nor to education, or proper employment, proper housing, clothing, food, water.

I do not go to school. But I do read everything I can get my hands on. My uncle Param, before he was killed, taught me how to read. More importantly, he instilled in me the value of reading and education. I still dream of leaving Trilokpuri. Even after last night.

Until yesterday, I worked with mother serving an upper caste family in New Delhi. House cleaning. Even though we'd scrub the place spotless every day, afterwards they'd still spray the rooms with disinfectant and holy water to purify all we had touched.

Each day, we'd travel to and from work on foot.

We do not own a car.

To ride the bus, we must board it last, and even then we are not allowed to sit in the seats even if they're unoccupied. We must stand. Which we would do but boarding the bus last usually means no room, not even to stand.

Dalits are not allowed to ride bicycles either. That would mean "polluting" the streets of the higher castes.

So we walk.

Barefoot.

Shoes are off limits to us too.

Mitesh remains at home, watched by old Jeevana, our neighbor. A sweet old lady who smells bad but means well.

At the end of each work day, mother and I would visit the

city dump where we would collect plastic bags from the piles of rotting waste there.

We need the plastic bags for water.

The tap near our home cannot be used by Dalits. Instead, we must walk a half mile down the road to the Dalit tap, the one in which the water barely trickles.

Drip-drop.

Drip-drop.

The sound is embedded in my ears at night. One tiny drop. Stop. Another tiny drop. Stop. It's maddening.

This is how we get our water. The water we use to cook, wash, and drink. And we bring it home in plastic buckets and bags we find in the dump.

Which is one of the reasons why Mitesh is so sickly.

"I don't want to die," he said to me yesterday.

"Nobody wants to die," I answered. "But we're all mortal. We don't last forever."

"You're making me sad."

"I didn't say you're going to die now."

"I feel like I am."

"Well, you're not. You're a boy. Boys grow into men. Men become old men. Old men die."

"Mahtab was a boy, and he died," Mitesh said.

Mahtab was Mitesh's best friend. Killed two years ago when he fell into a drum filled with chemical waste. The factory is closed now. It had been operating illegally. But another one will open to take its place, and there'll be more drums filled with illegal chemicals for children to fall into. That's life in Trilokpuri.

"Yes, Mahtab died. But Mahtab didn't have an older sister. I'm not going to let anything happen to you. In fact, I've got a plan to make you healthy."

"You do?"

"Yes."

"What is it?"

I slid across the dusty blanket and snuggled close to him. Close enough to whisper in his ear. "I know where I can find food. Lots of food."

"Where?"

"Over in New Delhi, there are fine restaurants. Restaurants that cook more food than their patrons can eat. At the end of the day, there's tons of food left over. Do you know what happens to this food?"

Mitesh shook his head.

"Well, by law, these restaurants can't serve the extra food the next day, so they throw it away. Guess where they throw it?"

"I don't know."

"In our dump. They dump it there in the middle of the night, and when they dump it, it's still fresh."

Mitesh frowned. "But mother says there's no food at the dump."

"Not in the daytime."

"So how are you—" His little eyes widened. "You can't go at night!"

"Why not?" I ask.

"You know! The butcher!"

"The butcher's in jail."

"But he gets out at night!" Mitesh exclaimed. "He prowls the streets at night and chops off people's heads!"

"No he doesn't."

"My friends—"

"Your friends like to tease you. You shouldn't listen to everything they say. Mitesh, when the butcher committed his crimes, it was a long time ago. I wasn't even born yet. He's locked up, Mitesh. He doesn't get out."

"Then who killed those people? The police really found those bodies without heads! I heard mother talking about it!"

That much was true. Several mutilated bodies of young people had been found recently in and around Trilokpuri. Bodies without heads, arms, even legs.

"I don't know who killed them, Mitesh. Probably somebody who's long gone by now. I'm going to the dump. At night. I'll be safe."

"How do you know? Did Kali tell you?"

"Kali doesn't actually talk to me, Mitesh. I read about her teachings, and she speaks to me through my thoughts."

"What does she say?"

"Oh, things like pain and death are not overcome by denying them, or by fearing them!"

"You're not afraid to die?" Mitesh asked.

"I'm not looking to die, if that's what you mean. But I'm not afraid of death, and I don't let fear of death stop me from doing the things in life I want to do."

"Like going to the dump at night?"

"Right."

"How can you like Kali?" Mitesh asked. "She looks like a monster."

"When have you seen Kali?"

"I've seen pictures of her in your books. I've seen her with all those heads around her neck, and her four arms, and she's always covered in blood! Yuck! And you say you love her?"

"Yes."

"Why?"

"Because she's truth."

"*She's* truth? What do lies look like?"

"Her appearance is symbolic, Mitesh. For example, those fifty heads around her neck represent the fifty letters of the Sanskrit alphabet."

Mitesh rolled his eyes. "Whatever."

"Kali is pure honesty. That's why she's my favorite goddess. She teaches that life is hard, full of pain, and then you die. To deny this is a waste of time. So don't deny it and don't be afraid of it! Live, is what Kali is saying! Sing, dance, shout! Do whatever you want! With Kali, we are free to live our lives the way we want to! No caste system! No restrictive rules! No fear that certain people will pollute you! No matter what you do, you will not live forever, so why make others suffer in the misguided hope that you will?"

"Is that why they hate us?" Mitesh asked. "Because they're afraid we'll make them die?"

"I don't know, Mitesh. Maybe."

Mitesh coughed. "I feel sick."

"Tomorrow morning you'll have a hearty meal. Tonight, I'll go to the dump—"

"Oh no you won't!"

I groaned.

"Mother! You're listening to my conversations again and being nosy and intrusive again!"

Mother limped from the shadows. Dragging her right leg, and with strands of gray hair dangling in front of her face, she looked like a sick old grandmother.

She was thirty-three.

"You are not going to the dump at night! It's too dangerous for a young lady! It's bad enough there are evil men out there," she coughed. "But at night—" Another cough. "You have to watch out for the Rakshasas!"

"There are no such things as Rakshasas!" I laughed.

"No? Then why have I seen them with my own eyes?"

"You've seen them?" I asked. "I don't think so! The Rakshasas are just stories created by others to keep us away from the things that will help us! There's fresh food being dumped out there every night! Food that is being taken by others because we've been told it's too dangerous to go out there, because some stupid ancient vampires haunt the roads at night! Whoever believes in such nonsense is crazy!"

"You believe in Kali," Mitesh observed.

"I believe in Kali as a spiritual being. As a symbolic inspirational being. Do I think Kali's out there patrolling the streets at night? No! And neither do I think there's Rakshasas out there! In fact I know there's not!"

"How do you know?" Mother asked.

"Common sense that's how!" I shouted.

"I know Rakshasas exist! I've seen them!" Mother said.

"Of course you've seen them. Right after you've guzzled some of Jeevana's special brew."

She slapped my face.

"Don't mock me! I tell you I've seen them! With their bull heads, bloated bellies, and funny little hands. Hands that are pointed backwards. And teeth! Teeth that eat human flesh! And you know what else they eat? Rotting food, exactly the kind you find at dumps! Which is why, young lady, you are not going there at night! Do you hear me, Dhara? Answer me!"

I swallowed what little spit was left in my mouth, and my pride.

"I hear you."

"You're not going to the dump! Understand?"

"Yes."

I know when it's time to be quiet. To give in.

Because I'm no different from any other sixteen-year-old girl, regardless of my social status.

I kissed mother good night, waited for her tired body to fall asleep, and went out anyway.

H-h-hoot. Hoot. Hoot.

Owls have a special place in Indian mythology. To hear an owl's hoot is considered a bad omen.

Last night, as I left my home, I heard one.

I don't believe in omens, so I dismissed it. Funny that I remember it now.

It was nearly midnight yet it wasn't dark. The moon was glowing nearly as brightly as the sun.

I reached the dump without incident and walked along the dirt path past the huge piles of refuse all around me, some so high I couldn't see the top. The smell, as always, was bad, particularly so on this warm June night, but I was used to it and didn't even hold my nose anymore.

The grounds were very familiar to me. I knew exactly where I was going.

I found the pile of crushed cans I was looking for, crouched behind it, and waited.

I had expected to see the place crawling with rats. I'd heard rats owned the dump at night. I was really surprised I hadn't seen any.

Within a half hour, the low hum of a truck engine rumbled in the distance. I peered out from behind the cans and saw two headlights heading towards me. A few minutes later, a large dump truck was spilling its contents onto the ground, creating a fresh pile, a pile I knew contained food. I knew because I could smell it.

I waited, and after the truck had driven away, I sprang for the booty.

The pile had everything. Steak, fish, rice, chicken, salad

greens, fruit, and the most enticing of all, the most mouthwatering fresh bread. The aroma made my knees wobble. If I hadn't been so happy, I would have been angry, to know that here we were starving, and they were putting food like this in the dump. But thoughts of Mitesh feasting on fresh bread in the morning stamped out any sparks of anger festering in my heart.

I had stuffed my pockets with the plastic bags mother and I had gathered for collecting water. I pulled out these bags and began to fill them, reaching first for some succulent looking rolls. They were still soft.

I worked quickly, stuffing as much food into the bags as possible. It would only take me a few minutes, and I'd be on my way back home.

I was busily working when from behind me, came a sound that made me jump. A grunt. Like an animal.

I froze. Paused to listen, and then, after a moment's hesitation, looked over my shoulder.

A figure stood next to the pile of cans I'd been hiding behind. I gasped.

It was a man, a large man, and the bright moonlight enabled me to see clearly his awkward shape. He had a potbelly and a round bald head with large pointy ears. He wore clothes that anyone in Trilokpuri might wear, but there was something abnormal about him. He stepped closer.

His eyes were like narrow slits, and he had a blatant overbite. His top teeth hung down below his lower lip.

Then I looked at his hands. His right was where his left should be, and vice versa.

Backward hands.

Rakshasas!

"What do you want?" I cried.

He raised his left arm and pointed the index finger of his right hand at me.

"You!"

My fingers clenched the two plastic bags I had filled with food.

"Why?" I asked.

"You are a Dalit! A pollution!"

"I'm not a Dalit!" I lied.

He flashed his teeth. "You *are* a Dalit. I can *smell* you!"

I dashed to my left. I was a fast runner. I didn't know what else to do but run away. But the plastic bags were heavy, and my whole body was shaking.

I could feel the heavy thumping of his feet behind me. Gaining on me. I screamed.

A powerful blow to my back propelled me through the air. I fell to the ground. The bags went flying. I scraped my knees and the palms of my hands on the rocky earth.

He pounced on top of me, flipping me over on my back. I fought him viciously. Scraping at his face, kicking and kneeing his groin. He hit me hard in the cheek, just to the right of my nose. I blanked out for a second. Felt singeing pain.

When my vision cleared, he had lowered his face towards mine to the point where he could have kissed me. I tried to move, but he had pinned my arms to the ground.

I spit in his face and kneed him in the crotch again. He merely smiled.

His fangs were huge and jagged. They looked like they could penetrate my flesh and tear it to shreds in a heartbeat.

I looked into his slanted eyes. They were devouring me. He was set to pounce for the kill. I believed I was going to die.

"Kali!" I cried. "Be with me now, please! Take me with you into the next life!"

The Rakshasas retracted his lips and scowled at me in disgust.

I remembered mother's words, how she always said the Rakshasas abhor any and all forms of prayer.

"Oh Kali! I pray to you! I love you!" I shouted.

He snarled and jumped away from me. I was about to utter every prayer I had ever learned when from the darkness came a great cry, a woman's cry.

"Kali!" I screamed.

The Rakshasas turned his head just as a broom handle slammed him in the side of his face. He groaned and fell backwards out of my sight.

I sat up to see Mother running towards me with a broom in

her hands. She grabbed me by the arm and lifted me to my feet.

"I'm sorry!" was the first thing I said. "I was getting food for Mitesh!"

"Did he bite you? Did he pierce your skin with his teeth?"

"No."

"Mercy! Run! Run!" She pushed me.

I stumbled away from her and the Rakshasas, and as I regained my balance, I remembered the reason I was out there in the first place—Mitesh's food!

I turned around.

Ran past mother, *towards* the fallen Rakshasas, because behind him, lay the plastic bags.

"Come back here!" Mother called. "You'll get us both killed!"

I passed the unconscious creature and reached down and grabbed the bags. When I had them firmly in my hands, I turned and couldn't help but glance at the ugly sleeping beast. He opened his eyes.

I screamed and charged towards mother. He rolled to his side and swiped at my feet. I leaped, and his backward hands missed their mark.

"Run, mother, run!" I shrieked, as I ran towards her and past her, with the two stuffed bags hanging below my knees.

For some reason mother was not running. I looked behind me to see her standing there, facing the charging Rakshasas.

"Come on, Mother!"

She raised her right hand, motioning for him to stop. The broomstick in her left hand was low to the ground, like a cane.

"Hit him with the broom!" I shouted.

She didn't. Instead, she started to pray aloud, and the Rakshasas skidded to a halt. I stopped running as well, remaining some distance behind mother.

"You cannot touch us," I heard mother say. "Not with prayer on our side."

The Rakshasas growled. Snarled. Threw obscene gestures our way. But he did not come any closer.

"Dhara," Mother said to me without looking back. "Go home, please."

"No, I don't want to!"

"Foolish woman," the Rakshasas said. "You cannot pray forever! You will tire."

"Dhara," Mother called again. "Go home!"

"I don't want to leave you alone!"

"That's right, little girl," the Rakshasas said to me. "You don't want to leave your mother alone with me."

"Don't listen to him, Dhara!" Mom warned. "Go home. Your brother needs you!"

"*Brother?*" the Rakshasas asked. His slanted eyes swelled open. "You have a son."

"No!" Mother groaned.

Even from where I stood, I could see in the Rakshasas' face that he was experiencing some vision. His eyes twitched as if in a momentary trance.

"At home," he said. "Alone."

He snickered.

He turned to his left and bolted from our sight.

Mother whirled around.

"Run, Dhara! Run home as fast as you can!"

I panicked. Froze.

"Go! Don't wait for me!" she cried, hobbling towards me, dragging her right leg. "And remember, a Rakshasas is powerless against prayer!"

I turned, gripped the bags tightly in my hands, and ran home as quickly as I could, leaving mom behind in the dust.

The bulky bags were slowing me down, I knew that. But the thought of not getting this food to Mitesh—I would not let my brother be denied! Yet, if I didn't make it home before the Rakshasas, Mitesh would be dead.

I didn't get the chance to debate this further.

Out of nowhere, on my right, a man charged at me. Knocking into me at full force.

I flew backwards through the air. The bags went flying. I screamed, just before hitting the ground with a thud. I landed flat on my back, and the back of my head hit the ground hard. I lay there for a few moments, and as the dust settled, I saw a man standing above me. It wasn't the Rakshasas. This man was taller, much less round, much more lean.

I sat up and grasped the back of my aching head. The moonlight shone on the stranger's face, and I recognized him immediately.

"Gurbachan?" I asked. "What are you doing out here?"

Gurbachan was one of the young men from the neighborhood. A Dalit. He often helped mother and me carry our bags of water back to our home.

He didn't answer.

"Help me up, please," I asked, stretching out my hand to him. "Mitesh is in trouble."

Gurbachan reached for me. I thought he was going to help me. Until I saw in his hand a knife. A big knife. The kind butcher's use.

The butcher!

Mutilated bodies without heads, some of them found right here in this dump.

"Gurbachan! What are you doing with that knife?"

He raised it over his head. I saw his eyes. He had predator eyes. He was going to kill me.

"No, Gurbachan!" I cried. "It's me! Dhara! You can't!"

His arm flinched, and I screamed.

"Dhara!" Mother called.

She was hobbling towards us, her chest heaving from exhaustion.

Gurbachan looked over his shoulder.

Without getting up, I kicked him in the backside, and he stumbled forwards, but he kept his balance.

"Watch out, mother! He's got a knife!"

Mother stopped and raised the broomstick in front of her body. Gurbachan regained control of his footing, while I jumped to my feet. He wielded the knife frantically in front of him, back and forth between mother and myself. I expected him to attack me since I had no weapon but instead he lunged at mother.

I screamed as Gurbachan grabbed the broom handle with his left hand and wrenched it from mother with almost no effort. He flung it into a pile of battered old furniture.

I charged them as fast as I could, but before I even took three steps, he had twirled mother around, wrapped his arms around her like a great bear, pulled her up close against his body, and raised the blade of the knife to her throat.

"Keep away!" Gurbachan warned me. "Or I'll cut her right now!"

I stopped short.

He shrieked.

Mother was biting his hand.

He ripped his hand from her mouth and slugged her in the side of the face.

"Gurbachan! Stop it!" I cried. "It's us, Gurbachan! We're your own!"

"No!" He screamed, reaffirming his grip on mother, keeping the blade of the knife pressed hard against her throat. "I'm not a Dalit! Not anymore! I'm my own man!"

"Dhara," Mother muttered from behind Gurbachan's grasp. "Go home. To Mitesh!"

"No, I won't leave you!"

"Please."

"Shut up! Nobody's going anywhere!" Gurbachan yelled.

"For me," she muttered again.

"Shut up!" Gurbachan roared. He punched mother in the ribs.

I cried out, "Leave her alone!"

I almost charged them, but I saw in mother's eyes that look, that imploring sincere look that was begging me to listen to her. To save myself and my brother. To save her children. And I knew then this is what she wanted most.

"For you," I said, fighting back tears.

She mouthed "thank you" without uttering a sound, and I turned and ran away as fast as I could, not looking back at mother or Gurbachan, not even once.

I ran hard, and I couldn't get away fast enough.

The image of my mother being slaughtered like an animal, her head and limbs hacked from her body by that maniac Gurbachan, a boy she had often invited into her home and fed, was nearly too much for my legs to bear, but the driving force that kept me going, that kept me running, was the worst most horrifying fear of all.

The fear I'd hear my mother's death screams.

"Please! Don't let me hear her scream!" I pleaded repeatedly.

I raised my hands to my ears to block out all sound, which was a bad idea, because it screwed up my balance and slowed me down.

But I knew—I *knew*.

There would be no escape.

At the sound of the first cry, I dug my fingers into my scalp while keeping my thumbs inserted in my ears. And I kept running.

The next shriek—I cannot describe. I will not describe it. I only pray that for the rest of my life I never hear anything like it again.

I fought to keep running. To block out the world and keep my legs moving.

But the cries continued.

There was a high-pitched wailing.

I stopped and uncovered my ears.

"Oh no! *Oh no!*" I shrieked.

It wasn't mother screaming anymore.

It was Mitesh.

I did an about-face and ran my burning emotionally drained body back to where I had left mother and Gurbachan, because that's where Mitesh's cries were coming from. I rounded a heaping pile of crushed cans and skidded to a stop.

Gurbachan and Mitesh were scuffling with each other, the madman towering over my emaciated brother. Mother's body was lying on the ground to their right.

Gurbachan thrust my brother to the ground and raised the butcher's knife high above his head.

"Gurbachan! Don't!" I shrieked.

He stopped and looked at me.

Then lunged at Mitesh.

Swoosh!

From behind Gurbachan a body flew through the air, grabbing him by his shoulders and wrenching him from his feet. The two bodies sailed over Mitesh and crashed to the ground to my left.

I raced to my brother and slid down next to him, wrapping my hands around his head, and I couldn't stop kissing his face. My hands touching him, feeling the warmth of his body, the softness of his skin, and my eyes seeing him alive and unharmed, I'd never felt more joy. I hugged him close.

"For you, mother," I whispered.

"Mother's dead," Mitesh whimpered.

I lifted his face and looked into his eyes, and I saw in his trembling distorted expression that he had seen what I had raced away not to see.

"Oh Mitesh," I said.

A guttural cry reminded me of the danger still with us.

The two figures, locked in a violent struggle, had risen to their feet. I recognized the newcomer immediately. There was no mistaking his awkward shape.

The Rakshasas.

He had wrapped his backward hands around Gurbachan's throat and was attempting to strangle the life out of him.

"The boy is mine!" he shouted at Gurbachan.

I covered Mitesh's eyes, but I watched as Gurbachan fumbled for his knife and plunged it mercilessly into the Rakshasas' chest.

It had no effect. The Rakshasas continued to strangle Gurbachan, and with his windpipe blocked and no air to breathe, Gurbachan weakened quickly, and he dropped his knife to the ground.

With my arms still wrapped securely around Mitesh, I helped him to his feet.

The Rakshasas jerked his head towards us.

"Where are you going?" he asked.

I had no answer.

"There's no escape for you!" he shouted.

"Why not?" I asked. "Eat him! He's a Dalit!"

Gurbachan glared at me with wild eyes.

"I'm not a Dalit!" he gasped.

The Rakshasas sniffed the top of Gurbachan's head. He grimaced. Then smiled. "Dalit."

"My brother and I have no quarrel with you!" I said to the

Rakshasas. "You have not harmed us tonight! But he has! He killed our mother!"

The Rakshasas snickered. "Good for him!"

"He has spilled the blood of many Dalits!" I continued. "Imagine what *his* blood must taste like!"

"Yes," the Rakshasas said. "Intriguing."

"Take him! Let my brother and I go!" I begged.

"Why take one when I can have *three*?" the Rakshasas asked.

"Because—I can give you more than three! Others like him!"

"Others? Explain."

"Trilokpuri is filled with people like Gurbachan who prey upon my people at night! Upon young girls like me. I'll be the bait for you."

"I need no help finding food."

"No? How many of those you feed upon are like him? You thrive on filth and disgust! I know you do! I will get you the most vile despicable members of my race! Just let my brother and I go, and I will do this for you!"

"You know me well. Well enough to know I cannot be trusted. I will turn on you. It is my nature!"

"It's the price I'm willing to pay for the safe return home of my brother and I tonight!"

"No, Dhara!" Mitesh whispered.

"Shh!" I said to him.

"I *will* turn on you," the Rakshasas said. "You're a fool to make this deal."

"I'm getting my brother home safely, that's not so foolish!"

The Rakshasas mulled over my words.

"Midnight," he said. "Tomorrow. Here."

"I'll be here," I said.

"Take the boy, and go," he said.

I grabbed Mitesh by the hand and ran. Out of the corner of my eye I saw the plastic bags filled with food on the ground. I left them there.

"There'll be other nights," I told myself. "Get Mitesh home."

I looked over my shoulder once.

To see the Rakshasas bury his head into Gurbachan's throat. There was a thunderous cry and even in darkness I could see the spray of blood. I looked forward and raced Mitesh home.

That was last night.

Where my life will go from here, I don't know.

This morning I dreamt again of Mitesh and I leaving Trilokpuri. I still believe in this dream. I still believe it will come true.

In a few hours it will be midnight.

But I'm not afraid.

Not of the Rakshasas.

Not of death.

I am a Dalit.

I am untouchable.

"Monster on His Back" is from 2002 and appeared in Edo Van Belkom's young adult horror anthology *Be Very Afraid*. This tale of a high school teen trying to ask out the girl of his dreams is "inspired by true events." Yep, I experienced some god-awful dating horrors back in the day, and while I've suppressed most of them, I did resurrect some for this story. I think the agony boys often go through trying to ask out a girl for the first time is universal and most teens I believe can relate to the events in this tale.

MONSTER ON HIS BACK

The girl of his dreams was in front of him.

Dodie Metcalf, the most beautiful girl in the school. The most beautiful-looking creature he had ever laid eyes on.

Behind him, riding on his back and looking over his shoulder, was the monster. The unseen creature who'd been haunting him for months, hounding him ever since he first realized he "liked" Dodie.

She's too good-looking for you, the monster said. *She'll never go out with you!*

"Leave me alone!" Roddy shot back, wading through the congested halls of New Bedford High School. Halls teeming with students, twenty-eight-hundred of them, all trying to reach their next class within three minutes.

It was the last day of school, and Dodie would be off to camp for the summer. It was now or never.

He caught up to Dodie and tapped her on the shoulder. "Hi, Dodie!"

She turned her head, her eyes meeting his. "Hi, Roddy," she said with a half-smile.

His knees wobbled. For a moment, he forgot how to breathe. Then, with a flourish, "Missed you yesterday in English!"

Oh, that was smooth!

"I stayed home. It's not like we're doing work anymore," Dodie said.

"That's true. We're not. Well, I just wanted to say—good-bye."

Idiot!

"And—um, wish you a good summer."

"Thanks. You have a good summer too."

"Thanks."

He was running out of time. Passing period was nearly over. A sudden drought parched his mouth; his tongue became swollen with a foul coating of anxiety. He couldn't speak.

Cat got your tongue? Heh, heh!

Why was it so difficult? Why did his tongue become a twisted pretzel every time he was with this girl? He wanted to scream. And why was it so loud? All around him, it was like a raucous crowd at a baseball game. How can a guy be expected to pose a romantic question in these surroundings?

He wished he was on a soap opera. Those guys had it easy. Wanna ask your dream girl out? Soap opera guy would have an entire restaurant reserved just for him and his woman, with hundreds of lit candles in the background and romantic music softly supporting every word. The surroundings would be so quiet that he could whisper and she'd still hear everything he had to say.

What did he have?

A school corridor filled to capacity with rowdy teenagers and only thirty seconds to make his pitch. While speed walking.

What chance did he have? What chance did any high-schooler have with a teasing, taunting monster on his back—one that wouldn't let him relax for a second?

Say something! Say it now—if you can! the monster roared.

"Dodie, I was wondering—Ow!"

Roddy stumbled backwards, was nearly knocked off his feet by a tall, lanky freshman overexcited about becoming a sophomore. The future basketball star had collided into Roddy, sending him crashing into a locker.

"Why don't you watch where you're going?" Roddy cried.

"Sorry, man!" answered the soon-to-be sophomore, never breaking his stride.

Weakling! Fall on your butt, why don't you?

Roddy rubbed his face in embarrassment, shielding his eyes from Dodie's gaze.

"Are you all right?" she asked and touched his shoulder.

He experienced a sudden surge of strength, brought on by the feel of her slender fingertips.

"Yeah. Freshmen! Anyway, Dodie, I was wondering—"

She looked him right in the eye. Her brown eyes were the most beautiful things he had ever seen.

Look at those eyes. They're perfect! You're out of your league.

"Shut up!"

"Excuse me?" Dodie asked.

"Er—nothing. I was wondering if—if maybe we'll get a chance—Do you think you'd—"

The bell rang.

That's it. Game over!

"Gotta get to class," Dodie said. "See you later."

She walked away.

What a loser.

"Dodie!" he called.

She stopped, turned around.

"Can I just—I know the bell rang, but it's the last day of school. Can I ask you something?"

"Sure," she said, approaching him.

Roddy's stomach churned like a flushing toilet and his face blazed like a furnace, dripping sweat down his temples and neck.

She can see you sweating!

He ignored the monster on his back. Ignored it as best he could, even as he knew she could see the embarrassment on his face, the wetness saturating his collar and shirt.

"You were talking about some new movie the other day, and I thought—I don't know—it might be fun if we went to see it together."

"You and me?" Dodie asked, her face brightening with a smile.

"Yeah. But we don't have to or anything if you're—you know, busy."

"When did you want to go?"

"How about tomorrow night?"

"Sure, why not?"

Roddy wasn't sure he'd heard her right. "What?"

"It might be fun." She paused, then said, "Look, I've got to go. We can talk more about this later."

A sense of calm flooded over Roddy, like cool, cool water.

And the monster, it seemed, had nothing to say.

"She said yes!" he shouted. "I'm going out with Dodie Metcalf!"

Big deal, said the monster.

"What are you still doing here?" Roddy asked. "You're supposed to be gone now."

Why?

"I asked her out. She said yes."

No, no. We're just getting started, Roddy, by boy!

"But I thought—"

You thought that if you asked your little cutie for a date, I'd go away? I'd be crushed by your small victory?

"Something like that."

Wrong! the monster snickered. *Tell me, Roddy, on Friday night, on your date, are you going to—hold her hand? Kiss her? What if you try and she refuses? Can you handle that? What if you tell a joke, and she doesn't laugh but rolls her eyes instead? What if you can't stop saying the same thing over and over again? What* will *you do?*

Roddy screamed.

And the monster laughed.

This one is from 2002 and was published at Horrorfind.com. The inspiration behind this tale was a true life event that happened to me when I was living in Boston in the early 1990s. I was walking home from my part-time job one night when a woman in front of me had her purse snatched, and I stupidly chased the guy into an alley. Lucky for me, when I got there, the guy had disappeared, and I went back and stayed with the woman until the police came. But for a moment there in that alley I feared something worse might happen. Something like—

A FLY ON THE WALL OF HELL

From the hole, blood seeped.

He clenched both his hands together over the gaping wound in his abdomen, praying he could prevent the precious drops of life fluid from spilling out onto the pavement.

He lay flat on his back in the middle of the darkened alley, wondering how he had gotten himself into this mess?

He had been walking home from his evening job as a clerk at Video Heaven, one of the city's larger video rental chains. It was well after midnight when he had begun his two-mile trek back to his apartment. Generally, he didn't fear walking home alone since he was a guy, and he figured a guy had less to fear on a darkened city street than a woman. He was right, even on this night when he had been shot in the abdomen, for it had been a woman, a half block in front of him who had had her purse snatched. He had run to her assistance, but she hadn't waited for it. She had pursued her assailant into the narrow stretch of pavement which ran between two brick apartment buildings, where no light was allowed entry.

Not smart.

Which left him, twenty-two-year-old Robbie Nanz, a first year high school teacher who had to work nights to pay his city rent, with no other choice but to follow her into the darkness. It certainly ran against his better judgment, but what else could he have done? Walked away? Not him. Not Mr. Responsible.

The alley was pitch black. He hadn't been able to see a thing. He had heard the woman's footsteps, and he had called out to her. The next thing he knew he was lying flat on his back on the alley floor. He had heard the loud pop of a gun, felt the burning pain in his gut, and had collapsed to the cement like a clipped weed. He wasn't even sure if it had been the purse snatcher who had shot him.

He was terribly afraid. He didn't want to die. He lay as still as he possibly could, keeping his two hands cupped over the moist cavity in his midsection. He knew he would need something more absorbent than his own hands to stop the bleeding. With his right hand, he gathered the abundant material of his over-sized shirt, scrunched it up, and pressed it into the raging wound.

He grimaced and ground his teeth, for the pain felt as if someone had taken a razor blade to his gut. He nearly passed out. Taking deep breaths, he overcame the pain and settled himself down.

He thought about screaming for help, but there was something secure about the blanket of darkness which enveloped him, and he didn't want to forfeit his only form of protection. For all he knew, his cries would summon the man who had shot him, and he'd return to finish the job. As things stood now, it was so dark he couldn't even see his own feet, thanks to his black sneakers, and so he seriously doubted anyone else in the alley could see him.

He wondered about the woman he had tried to assist. No longer could he hear her footsteps, or anything else for that matter. The night was momentarily silent.

Exhausted, he closed his eyes for a moment's respite.

A warm breeze screeched over his face. He opened his eyes. Something large flew across the sky.

Robbie blinked.

There it was again. The largest bird he had ever—more of them. Three, four—a half dozen! All flying by overhead. They looked to be the size of human beings, with a wingspan of what had to be twenty feet!

"I must be hallucinating," Robbie muttered.

Once more, the enormous flapping creatures soared across the nighttime sky, gliding effortlessly with their wings spread like majestic eagles, only six times the size.

"Am I going crazy?" he asked himself. "I'm not dreaming, I'm certain of that, and I'm pretty sure I'm not hallucinating. I mean, I feel coherent. But then how do you explain those things up there? For God's sake, Robbie, even if you were hallucinating, why the hell would you imagine giant birds?"

Footsteps, behind him. Slow and deliberate.

Snickering. A low "heh, heh, heh, heh."

He swallowed, suddenly feeling quite vulnerable.

The footsteps drew closer.

Robbie's forehead, already saturated with sweat, began to overflow with a deluge of fear-induced perspiration.

"What do I do? Shout? Stay still?"

Fear commanded that he take the second option.

The footsteps stopped.

In the distance, a woman's high heels clomping on the sidewalk, growing louder.

"Hey baby!" called a gruff male voice, hollow, as if heard through a phone line.

Silence.

A woman's laugh.

"You betcha!" The male voice again.

Robbie strained to hear. Suddenly, two sets of footsteps approaching him: the heavy boots of the man, and the loud heels of the woman. He felt his chest tighten as they drew nearer. He should have called out immediately, he knew, but this snickering man had unnerved him. He remained mute.

The footsteps passed him by without incident. The couple were now deeper in the alley.

Silence again.

Then the sound of heavy breathing. They were making out.

"Terrific!" Robbie thought. "I get to be a fly on the wall to this!"

"What are you doing?" the woman's voice asked.

"heh, heh, heh, heh."

"Stop it!"

The crack of a slap.

"No! Help!"

Robbie instinctively attempted to jump up, but the second he moved, searing burning pain shot through the hole in his abdomen, and he keeled over on his side.

The unseen struggle between the man and the woman was vicious and violent. The man was snarling like a wild animal. The woman managed one more loud scream before she was stifled into nothingness.

Robbie rolled onto his back again, still sweating from the combined effects of fever and stress.

The wind blew. No one else made a sound.

"heh, heh, heh, heh."

The man was still there. Robbie listened carefully. The man seemed to be—*slurping* something.

"Her blood," Robbie thought.

A faint—sobbing. The woman was alive!

"Okay, Robbie, get a hold of yourself! Perhaps it's nothing. Just kinky sex."

The woman squealed in pain.

"Still could be kinky sex," Robbie conjectured wishfully.

Then the words, whispered in agony, "somebody help me."

Robbie's fears were confirmed: this was not kinky sex. This was rape, or worse.

He was about to shout when something crashed to ground not three feet from where he lay.

He turned his head quickly to see in the darkness what looked like a smashed potted plant. Was someone from up above attempting to stop the rape? If they were, their efforts went unnoticed, for the rapist paid no attention to the crash, as he continued to suck and slurp.

"help me," squeaked a faint whisper.

Robbie inhaled, preparing again to shout when another sound distracted him once more.

A click. Like something settling in the floor inside a house late at night.

Robbie looked up at the apartment building wall which comprised the left side of the alley. He saw movement.

Something was climbing down the wall!

A man.

Crawling down the brick wall like Spiderman.

A loud belch, and Robbie turned his head towards the unseen rapist. He still could see nothing but darkness. He looked back at the wall: Spiderman was gone.

"All right, Robbie, take it easy! Stop shaking! What the hell is happening? What is all this shit? Why am I seeing all these weird things? People crawling down walls, birds the size of humans, these things don't exist! It must be the loss of blood. Oh God. I don't want to die! Don't let me die."

Robbie blinked. Once, twice, three times.

At first he wasn't sure, but the longer he stared, the more convinced he had become.

Not ten yards from him, by the wall, in front of what looked to be a trash can, stood a man.

Was it the man he had seen descending the wall? Or the rapist?

Someone else?

This man could have been a mannequin, he was *that* still. He stood erect, with his hands by his side. He seemed to be staring. At what, Robbie couldn't tell.

"heh, heh, heh, heh."

The cackling laugh. The man who had attacked the woman. Was that him standing there motionless in the darkness?

No.

The devilish laugh was coming from further down the alley.

Robbie heard footsteps again, approaching him. It wasn't the motionless man. He remained as still as dead.

"heh, heh, heh, heh."

The cackle was growing louder, closer.

Robbie swallowed, the sweat perspiring down his forehead

and through his armpits like the deluge of rain he expected
any moment from the angry clouds above him. His wound
throbbed, and he squirmed unintentionally.

The footsteps stopped.

Robbie's eyes left the motionless man and turned to his
right. Another figure was standing above him.

"heh, heh, heh, heh."

Robbie's eyes widened. The snickering man was enormous.
He had a body like Fat Albert and hands the size of catcher's
mitts.

A sliver of moonlight shot through an opening in the clouds,
and for a moment, Robbie could see the man's face.

It was chock-full of facial hair. His wide sideburns ran from
his ears to his chin. The hair on the top of his head was long and
scraggly. His bottom teeth were crooked and protruded from
his mouth like a set of bleachers.

Blood stained his lips.

"Get away from me," Robbie muttered.

The man was breathing heavily, as if exhausted. His boots
were now less than an inch from Robbie's forehead. He looked
down upon Robbie and his furry face grinned satisfyingly, as if
he had found new prey.

The man uttered something that Robbie didn't make out
at first, something that sounded like "bed," but when the man
spoke again, there was no mistaking what he had said.

Blood.

"More blood," the man growled, his words so rough they
were nearly incoherent, but Robbie heard them all the same.

"More blood!" the man said again, as he looked up towards
the moon.

And *howled.*

"Jesus Christ!" Robbie cried out.

Out of the darkness from above, a man leapt, crashing down
upon Robbie's attacker.

Robbie watched in disbelief as the being who had leapt from
the wall wrapped his long arms around the burly snickerer's
throat, and squeezed relentlessly. The furry man choked and
coughed, while his antagonist, sporting an amazingly athletic

build, dragged him towards the wall from which he had leapt.

Keeping his left arm locked on his victim's throat, he reached up with his long right arm towards the brick barrier which shielded them from the outside world. There was a grunt, and suddenly this mysterious athlete was climbing again, this time *carrying the hulking bloodmonster with him*, who all the while was struggling like a bear in a net.

"Unbelievable," Robbie muttered, as he watched the two men ascend the wall, so high that they disappeared from view.

A cry of pain. More than that. A death cry. Echoing throughout the entire alley.

Robbie nearly threw up. He turned his head and gave a start. By the trash can. The motionless man still stood. A faceless silhouette in the shadows.

"Who are you?" a trembling Robbie called to the dark statue. "Say something! Move! Help me!"

The figure remained as stone.

Robbie sobbed, closed his eyes, and lost consciousness.

When the doctor had finished his examination, Robbie finally was able to ask all the questions he had pent up in his mind. He learned that he had been brought in to the hospital that morning, that he had been unconscious for the better part of a day, and that he had sustained a serious bullet wound to the abdomen, but he had been found in time and the surgery had been a success: he was going to live.

"When they found me, was I alone?" Robbie asked.

"Yes."

"You wouldn't believe the things I saw in that alley."

"I have a pretty good idea."

Surprised, Robbie looked at the doctor tentatively.

"You've been talking in your sleep. The things you've gone on about!"

"What did I say?"

"Oh, the kind of things that aren't uncommon for a man in your condition. Delusions of that sort are quite normal. You see, when you lose a lot of blood, it's very traumatic on the brain, it causes it to panic, and it produces the kinds of hallucinations you experienced last night. But the good news is, you're here now, we've stopped the bleeding, and you should be able to enjoy a good night's rest. Give us a ring if you experience any more of those nightmares. We'll give you something to help you sleep."

"Thank you, doctor."

No sooner had the doctor left the room, when another voice spoke to Robbie: "Those weren't hallucinations."

Robbie turned his head to his right, to the man lying in the bed next to him.

"Excuse me?"

The man, who appeared to be in his mid-sixties with a bloated weather-worn face and big bushy eyebrows, lifted his head and addressed Robbie once more. "The things you saw last night. I heard you today, going on in your sleep about them. The doc was wrong. They're not hallucinations."

"How do you know that?" Robbie asked, and as soon as he had said the words, he believed he had found the answer. Behind the man, posted on the wall high above his bed, was a white sheet of paper with the words: "Bernie Kemper. Alcoholic. Do Not Give This Man Alcohol."

The man's eyes followed Robbie's. "Yes, I'm an alcoholic. That's why they leave me alone. Because nobody listens to a drunk."

"That's why who leaves you alone?"

"The creatures you saw last night. They're real. You're not a street person, are you?"

"No!"

"That's why you didn't know. Those of us who sleep on the streets know the rules."

"What rules? What the hell are you talking about?"

"The rules of the night life. You don't look at them, chief. When they come by, you close your eyes or look away and pray they leave you alone, 'cause if you don't, they'll make you pay. Do you know how many friends I've lost who tried to be brave, tried to show off that they could look and live? Too many!"

Robbie had turned away. He didn't believe this guy, and he wasn't enjoying listening to him.

"I know you don't believe me. Why should you? I'm just a drunk. But believe me, chief, at night, when you and the rest of your normal friends are asleep in your warm cozy beds, there's a whole other world out there which exists only from sundown to sunup. Night creatures rule the streets. I don't mean to ruin your evening, but you're in trouble, chief. You saw them. You didn't close your eyes. You broke the rules."

"Why don't you just shut up, all right? I don't want to listen to you anymore!"

"Tonight, when the sun goes down, they're coming for you. They're gonna make you pay."

"Shut up! Nurse! Nurse!"

"It won't do you any good, calling them. They can't help you."

"They can get you the hell out of here, that'll help me!"

"It'll help me too, chief. You think I want to be here when *they* come looking for you?"

"*Nurse!*"

The hospital was full, and to both Robbie's and Bernie Kemper's regret, there existed no extra space in which to move either one of them. They were stuck together.

Robbie had just dozed off when he was awakened by the rustling of the curtains. He opened his eyes and felt the warm summer breeze blowing across his face: the curtains were flapping back and forth like a flag atop a ship's mast.

He glanced at Kemper in the bed next to him: the man was clenching his eyes shut.

A click from the window.

Robbie gasped.

The long athletic arm of the wall climber swung through the open window, followed by his entire body. He landed softly on his feet, standing well over 6' tall.

Robbie twisted his upper body to reach for the button to summon the night nurse, and as he did so, he could hear the intruder's oncoming footsteps. The figure's ominous shadow enveloped the wall in front of him.

A hand grasped Robbie by the back of the neck, ripping him

away from the button, shoving him back onto the bed.

Robbie looked up at the intruder, seeing his face for the first time. It was as black as coal. No eyes, nose, ears or mouth. Just smooth blackness, until a red dot appeared where his mouth should have been, a red dot that quickly enlarged into a moist red ball.

Like a jack-in-the-box, a long protrusion catapulted out of the ball towards Robbie's throat.

"Jesus!" Robbie cried.

The protrusion stung him in the neck, and then the sucking began.

Robbie struggled, but to no avail. The deadly night creature had pinned him to the bed, sucking his blood like a giant mosquito.

"*NO!*" Robbie screamed, but to his surprise, he had no voice. The stinger in his neck had inhibited his vocal chords.

He looked over at Kemper: the man was still clenching his eyes shut.

"I don't want to die! I don't want to die!" Robbie exclaimed to himself, nonetheless feeling the pain of his life being drained from him.

A loud pop, and the climber's protrusion returned to its mouth. Robbie swallowed: he was still alive.

The intruder bent over the bed and lifted Robbie like he was a child, carrying him towards the window.

Robbie wanted to resist, but with so little blood left in his veins, his energy was practically nil.

Once the climber had reached the window, he hoisted Robbie through its opening.

Robbie looked down: he was twelve stories high.

"Oh God!" he cried to himself. "Why is this happening to me?"

The climber maneuvered so that he was holding Robbie's entire body out of the window, while his own body remained inside the hospital room.

Without warning, he let go.

The powerful rush of cold air stinging his face smothered Robbie as he felt his stomach sever from his intestines and ride up his throat through his mouth into the sky above him; at least that's what it felt like.

Robbie shrieked, knowing that the pavement was seconds away from splattering his body to smithereens.

A sharp pain stabbed him in the back of the neck, and suddenly he realized he had reversed direction: he was going up.

He looked over his shoulder and gasped at the sight of two talons embedded in the flesh behind his neck.

It was one of the giant bird creatures he had seen flying high above the alley last night. One of those creatures had just saved his life. It soared higher and higher, and when Robbie looked down, he saw that they were flying above the city's downtown area. The view made him nauseous. He wouldn't look down again.

But he would look up. To get a better look at his savior.

Perhaps what he had assumed to be some sort of beast was an angel of God.

He looked up at the magnificent flying creature.

"*No!*" Robbie wailed.

This savior was no angel of God. On the contrary, it was some sort of devil. Its entire body resembled a giant bird of prey, with the exception of its chest and head. It possessed the muscular bare torso of a man, a well-built man, and its face was the most hideous thing Robbie had ever seen in his life. Its flesh was withered and decrepit, its teeth rotted like a corpse's, and its eye sockets were black and hollow. It smelled of feces.

It turned its head, saw that Robbie was looking at it, and cawed like a hungry raven.

Robbie gasped and immediately sucked in the salt water aroma of the ocean. Against his better judgment, he looked down once more. The flying devil had carried him away from the city and was flying over the harbor heading towards the beach, for he could see the rocky banks in the distance.

The talons opened.

Robbie fell.

Shrieking, he closed his eyes and prayed for God's mercy.

He lost consciousness.

When his body hit the large wet rocks on the beach below, he didn't feel a thing.

He was already dead.

A horde of the hungry flying devils quickly descended upon him. The six beasts wasted no time picking at his split open insides. Feasting on his flesh, blood, and internal organs.

The ocean wind whipped and howled. In the distance, a bell on a buoy clanged, and even farther, the foghorn of a lighthouse groaned.

At the top of the beach, where the sand met the boardwalk, a solitary figure stood alone. Watching the winged devils devour their prey. The ferocious wind rocked everything on the beach, but the observing figure swayed not one inch. In fact, he did not move a muscle. He stood and he watched.

When the last intestine had been devoured, the massive creatures of the air again took flight, returning to the city skyline.

The solitary figure dressed in black remained on the boardwalk. Looking at the area where Robbie's bloody carcass lay.

In his hospital bed, lying flat on his back, with his eyes shut tightly as if sewn together, Bernie Kemper mutters, "They make you pay. You break the rules, they make you pay!"

The wind dies down.

On the horizon, the first rays of the morning sun.

The wet rocks, bloodless and clean.

The motionless figure gone.

I wrote this next story in the late 1990s when I was fed up with the Jerry Springer-type daytime talk shows. This is the first time this one is seeing print, as it's making its debut here in the pages of this collection.

WEIRDOS WHO WANT TO BE PARENTS

"Cue applause—fade music—ok, Jimmy, you're on!"
    "Good morning and welcome to the Jimmy Morganstern Show!" greeted the smiling forty-five-year-old daytime talk show host. "Glad you could join us. Do we have a show for you! Ready for this one? 'Weirdoes Who Want To Be Parents.'"

Cheers and howls boomed from the audience.

Jimmy Morganstern nodded approvingly, continuing to smile, satisfied that he was giving his audience exactly the kind of programming they wanted. And why shouldn't he have thought this? "The Jimmy Morganstern Show," now in its seventh season, was currently the top-rated daytime television series for the second year in a row.

"And did I mention that we're broadcasting *live* this morning?" Morganstern beamed, pushing his wire-framed glasses higher on his nose, as the crowd cheered again, glasses that served no other purpose than to make him appear intelligent and sensitive, for Morganstern was blessed with twenty-twenty vision.

"That's right, a live broadcast," Morganstern continued, his flowing blonde hair, which was obviously colored, glistening under the studio lights. "And the reason for this venture? The answer in a bit, but first, let's get the ball rolling and meet our guests."

On cue, Morganstern swiped his microphone, scurried into his studio audience, and twirled around to face the stage.

"I've got my dancing shoes on!" he sang jovially. "All right, weirdoes who want to be parents, let's hear from you. First we have Ron and Pat."

The camera switched to the stage, as Morganstern continued speaking off camera.

"As you can see, Ron and Pat are a rather obese couple who collectively weigh over 1,000 pounds!"

The audience booed loudly in disapproval.

"Ron and Pat are planning to have children. Specifically, they're planning to have fat children!"

More booing as the words "Ron and Pat, Want to have Fat Children" were superimposed over the television screen.

The enormous couple, Ron with slicked back greasy hair and dark-framed glasses, and Pat also with glasses and a sleeveless shirt that exposed her flabby blob-like arms, nodded in acknowledgment, appearing as relaxed and as comfortable as if they had just been announced as two human beings with dignity rather than as obese objects with peculiar views.

The camera moved along to the next guest, a gentleman of more moderate size, with short dark hair, graying about the edges, with a thick mustache and a serious expression that screamed, "don't mess with me!"

"Next we have George, a convicted rapist who's served his time and is now a free man again," Morganstern's voiced-over words explained. "George would like to adopt a child or find a surrogate mom. He wants to raise a child of his own and says his past record, if held against him, would be discriminatory."

"George. Former rapist. Wants to raise a child," said the superimposed scripted words, as the audience remained strangely quiet and subdued.

Sitting next to George, an extremely well dressed man, wearing an expensive suit, sporting a neat short haircut, and looking as self-righteous as a church minister.

"This is Stanton Forrester," Morganstern said. "Mr. Forrester is a member of the Ku Klux Klan, and it is his view that it is okay to raise children as white extremists."

The audience awoke from its temporary stupor with a new round of boos. Forrester nodded his head but said nothing.

"Cindy is our fourth guest," Morganstern continued as the camera moved on to the young woman with the full figure, short leather skirt, and a face that seemed tired and old for one who had not yet seen her thirtieth birthday. "Cindy is a prostitute. She claims her profession is ideally suited for someone raising children. I can't wait to hear her explanation."

Several in the audience chuckled.

"I can't wait to tell you!" Cindy exclaimed.

"And last but not least we have Joel," Morganstern said, reaching the guest he was most excited about.

The camera fell upon Joel, a solidly built young man with dark brown hair and rather good looking features, the first of the six guests on the stage who actually appeared somewhat nervous. His nose was twitching, and his face had the look of someone waiting outside a dentist's office.

"Joel doesn't know this, but he's the reason why we're doing this show live," Morganstern announced, as the camera provided a tight shot of Joel's face, catching his nose twitching three more times in quick succession. "You see—, Joel claims to be—*a werewolf.*"

The audience laughed.

"He—" Morganstern paused as he too chuckled, "—he is going to explain to us this morning I'm sure why someone who believes himself to be a werewolf would make a good parent, but that's not the reason why I'm so ecstatic about having Joel on this show. As those of you who watch us enough know, and have seen what we do around here on the days leading up to Halloween, I'm a huge fan of the supernatural! So, when one of my guests claims to be a werewolf, it's red carpet time! For you and me, that is, not for him! See, we're live today because at the end of this program—and this is the first time Joel's hearing about this—we're going to challenge him to transform on stage, in front of millions of television viewers, and if he can do it, this being a live broadcast, it will prove once and for all that things of the dark routinely dismissed as phony and kid's fare, like werewolves and vampires, really do exist! So, officially, our topic today is parenting, and during most of this hour that's what we'll be talking about, but don't you dare change the channel! Not before you see what Joel might do for us this morning. Hold on to your hats! It could be the thrill ride of your life!"

The audience roared, as the words, "Joel, Claims to be a Werewolf, Wants to Raise Children," were projected onto television screens nationwide.

The camera panned across the cheering audience, and when the applause subsided, returned to the always effervescent Morganstern.

"Okay, let's get this party rolling! As usual, we'll hear from each guest, and then we'll open it up for your questions and phone calls. Let's start with Ron and Pat."

The camera switched to the obese couple.

"You say you want to raise your children to be fat," began the unseen Morganstern as the camera remained on the seated couple. "Why would you want this when it's a medical fact that being overweight is extremely unhealthy?"

"Let me start by saying," Ron said in a rather feminine high-pitched voice, "that to Pat and I, being overweight is a form of beauty. There's nothing wrong with being heavy. Nothing to be ashamed of. Fat isn't a dirty word."

"Yes, but to raise your children to be fat, isn't that a bit extreme?" Morganstern questioned, trying his best to sound professional.

Ron shook his head. "No. We don't think so."

"That's because your head's too fat! You can't think!" heckled a man in the audience.

A quick shot of Morganstern rolling his eyes as Ron said, "I'm not even going to respond to that."

"Jimmy," Pat jumped in, "it all comes down to building character. We live in a difficult society. A dog eat dog world. Children need every advantage, and if a child is fat, and can learn to handle the adversity that goes along with it, having to hear things said to them like that man just said to us, then that child is going to be better for it."

"Shut up you fat cow!" another man shouted, as the crowd erupted in a loud throng of boos.

"It's true!" Pat said, her right eye quivering, as she realized by their angry gesticulations and finger pointing that the crowd's displeasure was aimed at her rather than at the hecklers.

"All right, let's move on to George," Morganstern said, as the camera returned to him. He looked down briefly at his set of index cards and then back up at his guest. "George, you've served your prison term for rape. You've done your time. Why not just find a job and start anew? Why come on this show demanding that you be able to adopt a child?"

The camera dissolved to George, who looked about as warm and cuddly as a tarantula.

"I am an American citizen. It is my right to raise children if I so desire, and anyone who denies me that right, based upon my prior record, is discriminating against me. That's wrong, and I won't stand for it," George said directly.

"Yes, but, and I hate to open this can of worms against you," Morganstern said, on camera again, looking once more at his index cards, "but weren't you convicted of raping a ten-year-old girl?"

The camera gripped George's face with a tight close-up, as the audience finally chose to boo at someone else other than a pair of 500 pound pacifists. The man didn't flinch.

"That was then. This is now. I love children."

An explosion of boos shook the studio, but George refused to be rattled. He simply raised his voice to be heard over the crowd and said, "You can't judge a man based on one mistake!"

When the camera returned to Jimmy Morganstern, he was smiling. "Next we have Stanton Forrester. Mr. Forrester, as an active member of the Ku Klux Klan, you want to raise your children as white extremists. Why?"

Stanton Forrester smiled smugly. "Jimmy, there is one pure race in this country, and everyone, regardless of what they may say in public, knows in their heart who that race is. The rest of the country is a disease. A walking disease. Like any parent, I want my children to be blessed with good health. I simply see my views as an extension of good health care."

"So, in effect, what you're saying is, you would like your child to look upon a black child, for instance, as a diseased individual?" Morganstern asked. "As someone to be spurned?"

"Yes," Forrester answered, to a new round of boos. "When you come to a red light, Jimmy, you stop your car. You don't go through the light. If you do, you're breaking the law. That's the way things are. It's the same with people. Except with people you're bowing to God's natural law, rather than man's law."

The camera caught Morgarnstern shaking his head. "Let's move on to Cindy. Cindy, you claim that your lifestyle as a prostitute is ideal for raising children. Now, I'm a liberal guy, but, come on!"

"It's not so far-fetched, Jimmy."

"It isn't?"

"No. First of all," Cindy said, "I make a lot of money. My child will be well provided for. Also, I work at night, and so I'd be home during the day. I'd be able to spend this time with my child. At night, while I'm at work, I'd hire a responsible person to sleep at my house. It's cheaper than day care."

"When would you sleep?" Morganstern questioned.

"On the job," Cindy answered. "Men don't last all night, Jimmy, and whoever thinks that, is dreaming!"

The audience laughed.

"And now for Joel," Morganstern said, nearly licking his lips in anticipation. "Joel, you claim to be a werewolf. Why in the world would someone who claims to be a werewolf think it's a good idea to be a parent?"

The camera switched to Joel, who by far looked the most nervous of the odd lot on stage. The young man shifted in his seat.

"I don't want to be a parent," he said.

Morganstern's eyes nearly did somersaults. "You don't want—then what are you doing on this show?"

"It was the only way for me to get on," Joel said, now beginning to shake. "I want—I want to kill you."

The audience gasped, but Morganstern laughed.

"You want to kill me? Why?"

"Because I *hate* you. I *hate* your show. I *hate* the way you take advantage of people, the way you allow people who have no right speaking even in public let alone on television access to a nationwide audience."

"Well, Joel, I don't know what to say, other than, welcome to America! Freedom of speech, you know? Freedom of choice! You're free *not* to watch! Nobody's forcing you to watch my show! And if you really want to do something about it, you're free to start your own show!" Morganstern said. "But I must tell you, you're in the minority. Americans love my show. They're watching in record numbers, and you know why? Because I'm giving them what they want!"

"People want drugs, too, but we don't give pushers daytime Emmy awards," Joel said.

"No, we don't, but—before I respond to Joel, let me just remind everyone that this is not a publicity stunt. I had no idea Joel was going to say these things. If I had, he wouldn't be sitting up there. Nonetheless, let me get this straight, Joel. Your answer to this problem, the problem being my show, is for you to come on during a live broadcast—and murder me? Don't you think that's a bit hypocritical? I mean, talk about sensationalistic television that's harmful. You can't get any lower than a televised execution! Aren't you smart enough to realize that you're being a hypocrite?"

"I have tried everything," Joel said, his voice full of desperation. "I've written you, petitioned your show, called my congressmen. Nothing. No results. You travel with an army of security guards. You even employ one who lives in your home. This is the only way I had to get close to you."

"Well, now that you're close to me, I have to admit, I'm delighted! I hope, for my ratings' sake, that you intend to attempt your threat against me as a werewolf?"

Joel's face hardened, erasing all traces of boyhood from his twenty-one-year-old visage. "When I'm through here," he uttered menacingly, "talk show hosts across the nation will think twice about who they put on television. When I'm through here, I will have scared the living hell out of every last one of you!"

"By all means, Joel, scare us to death, but do it quickly, will you? It's almost time for a commercial!" Morganstern winked.

Joel frowned. "You're not taking me seriously!"

"On the contrary, Joel, I'm taking you very seriously. I told you, you're the reason we're broadcasting live, today. We *want* to see you change. Unfortunately, it is time for a commercial, but if you want to change now, just say the word, and we won't go anywhere!"

"Am I on camera right now?" Joel asked.

"Is he—yes, you're on," Morganstern said. "And again, if I may, to our audience at home, we're coming to you live. What you're about to see will be without the benefit of special effects, make-up, or camera tricks."

Joel looked directly into the camera pointed at him. "To every parent watching this show, take your children away from the TV or change the channel. To you kids watching this without adult supervision, shut it off. Change the channel. Do it! Now!"

He took a deep breath and said, "God, forgive me for what I'm about to do."

He looked down at his lap, and for a moment, he sat there, as peaceful as a priest in prayer.

But when he returned his gaze to the camera, there was a hunger in his eyes that did not belong to a human being but an animal. He screamed, jolting the audience, a horrific cry, as if someone were severing his hand from his wrist without use of anesthesia. Like a kernel of corn, his face popped into something completely different. Whereas a second before he had been a man, now he was a werewolf.

A creature completely devoid of fear.

His face had changed completely. His ears had elongated, his nose had darkened into a wet snout, and his eyes had narrowed into thin slits of ferocity. Drool poured forth from his mouth and oozed down the front of his hairy chin, his entire head covered with wolf hair.

His physique retained the shape of a man, although his arms and chest had increased in size to the point where they were bulging from his snug shirt. His fingernails had sprouted into curled claws.

He looked to his right, at the full figured call girl, and snarled.

Cindy screamed, while George exclaimed, "Jesus!" The two of them, along with Stanton Forrester jumped from their chairs and quickly scrambled towards the rear left stage exit. Ron and Pat remained in their seats, leaning as far away as possible, knowing they'd never be quick enough to get out of the creature's path.

The werewolf snarled again, hurling its chair backwards across the stage before leaping at the stunned yet glowing talk show host. The entire studio audience screamed in unison.

"Now!" Morganstern hollered over the clamor.

A horde of security personnel poured onto the scene from every corner and crevice in the studio, and before the werewolf could continue its advance, several of these uniformed guards had crashed down upon the creature and had pinned him to the ground. Within three seconds, a dozen more men were on top of the beast.

The camera remained fixed to the free-for-all, interrupted only by a quick shot of Morganstern adjusting his glasses on his nose, watching the scuffle with interest. Behind him, the terrified faces of his invited audience.

When next seen, the werewolf was brandishing a large bloody bruise on its forehead. Cuffs had been slapped onto its hands.

Quickly, the army of agents whisked the beast backstage.

The camera returned to the beaming Morganstern.

"To everyone who's been watching this, both in the studio and at home, I'm speechless! We've just witnessed the most amazing spectacle I've ever seen! A man, a human being, just transformed himself before our very eyes into a werewolf! Again, we're live, here. What you just saw was the real thing! No special effects or camera tricks. Do you realize what this means? We have just proved that the supernatural exists! This broadcast is as historic as—"

From backstage, another hideous scream.

The camera jumped to the stage where a human arm flew across the set, landing on poor screaming Pat's lap. The woman shrieked and bounced and vomited all over herself, as the arm fell to the floor in front of her kicking feet.

"Oh my God! Go to commercial! Go to commercial!" the unseen director shouted.

"Don't you dare, Neil!" Morganstern shouted into his microphone. "Keep those cameras rolling!"

The werewolf leapt back onto the stage, the steel handcuffs still around its wrists, but the chain broken, and its hands free. Its lips, teeth, claws, and shirt were saturated with blood not its own. It snarled menacingly before once more charging across the stage towards the audience, towards Morganstern.

The camera followed the werewolf as it jumped from the stage and landed but a few yards in front of Morganstern, who reached into his suit jacket and pulled out a handgun, which he fired immediately, three times in rapid succession, hitting the werewolf in the chest, propelling the flailing beast backwards.

The werewolf crashed into the edge of the stage and then collapsed to the floor.

For several moments, Morganstern remained fixed in one position, his arm extended, his finger still wrapped around the trigger, his eyes staring straight ahead.

Dropping his arm to his side, he finally stepped towards the fallen creature. He looked down at the motionless beast on the floor, and again for several moments remained fixed in the same position, as if waiting for the thing to return to its human form. It didn't.

Morganstern looked directly into the camera.

"I may be controversial. I may be shameless. But I'm not stupid, and when a guest claims he's a werewolf, whether I believe him or not, I make sure I've got me a gun loaded with silver bullets! Is there a doctor in the audience? I'd like to make sure our friend here is dead."

A man scurried down to the front of the auditorium and knelt by the fallen werewolf's side. He felt for a pulse.

"He's dead," the doctor announced.

"Neil," Morganstern said to his unseen director. "You'd better call 911 and then send someone backstage to check on the guards. Neil? Are you there?"

"*You're fucked, Jimmy!*" Neil shrieked hysterically. "*We're all fucked!*"

"Keep your shirt on, Neil."

"Don't tell me to fucking keep my shirt on! We just televised a fucking bloodbath!"

"Neil, it's going to be all right. Trust me."

"Trust you? You're outta your fucking mind, trust you! We're all going to fucking jail!"

"Jail, Neil?"

"You just fucking shot someone! You fucking maniac!"

"Just keep the camera on me, Neil," Morganstern said, turning to look directly into the camera. He smiled. "Just having a conversation with my director. It's a good thing you can't hear what he's saying. He's not a happy camper right now."

Morganstern drew a deep breath and let it out to recompose himself.

"You have just witnessed an historical broadcast. I'm not talking about the live execution you just saw, although that in itself is remarkable in that we did it here, on this show, live. I'm talking about that man's assertion, yes, that man behind me lying in a pool of blood, his assertion that he was a werewolf. You saw it here, live, just a few minutes ago. A human man, looking as normal as you and me, changing before your very eyes, into a beast. A beast from the dark ages. For years, we've been fascinated by such stories, stories that just never seem to go away. In fact, they're so prevalent that most horror editors these days don't even want to see a story about a werewolf or a vampire, let alone read one! Why don't these stories go away? The answer to this question, I believe, is that these creatures are real. There can no longer be any doubt."

Morganstern looked over his shoulder and pointed to the body on the floor.

"That man really changed into a werewolf, and I really shot him with a silver bullet, and killed him!

"This is exactly what you the American people have been waiting for! You, who have enjoyed horror so faithfully over the years, now have the proof you need to truly be scared! Once and for all, we have proven here on this show that the supernatural exists! If you weren't afraid of things that go bump in the night before, you will be now. Let me repeat myself: the supernatural, werewolves, vampires, exist! And so, before we cut to a much-needed break for a commercial, let me say this: to everyone out there watching me, believe in the weird and the unexplainable! Believe! If it's out there, even in the form of rumor or legend, it exists! Believe!"

Beads of sweat had formed upon Morganstern's brow. He removed a white handkerchief from the inside pocket of his suit jacket and wiped the moisture away. Then he smiled.

"And don't forget to join us tomorrow for *Brothers Who Spank Their Sisters*. We'll have a preview later in this broadcast. *The Jimmy Morganstern Show*. Giving America the television it wants to see. We'll be back in a few minutes. Stay with us."

"Cue music—let's have a close-up of the dead werewolf—zoom into the bullet wound—fade to commercial—"

This story germinated from a recurring nightmare I used to have as a child, where an elephant and a bison would enter my bedroom and tickle me. How weird is that? Anyway, the story makes its debut right here, right now.

CAROUSEL ANIMALS

There's a fine line between fun and terror.

The child, a girl no older than six, in pigtails and wearing pink shorts and a butterfly tee shirt stained with blotches of melted chocolate ice cream, flailed her arms and kicked her legs, fighting off her mother with the ferocity of a wild animal. You might have thought the woman was trying to throw the girl into a raging fire. All this drama, all this pain, just to get the child to ride the carousel.

Terry shook his head. He had seen this scene play out many times before, kids fighting their parents, refusing to go on rides, while their moms and dads forced them on, all in the name of fun. He saw it nearly every day. It was his summer job, operating the rides at Rollins Rock Amusement Park. It was a small park as these places go, but it was a short drive from his home, and it paid well. Something to do to fill out his summer vacation before he went back to college for his senior year. Soon, he'd be looking for a real job, and since at twenty-years-old, he still had no idea what he wanted to do with his life, this thought terrified him.

The little girl shrieked.

"Keep screaming, kid," Terry thought. "It only gets worse."

"You love the merry-go-round," the mother said.

The child disagreed. She socked her mother in the eye.

"Ouch!" Terry said, feeling the woman's pain.

"I *hate* this ride!" the girl shrieked.

The mother lost it. All life left her face. It was as if one moment she was there, having fun at the amusement park, and the next she was at a funeral. Her eyes went dead, for a moment, before welling up with tears. She grabbed her daughter like a football and whisked her away from the ride.

"It's about friggin time!" said a man in line with a big head and a bigger belly. "If that were my kid—"

Terry tuned him out. He let the line of people file past him so they could make their way onto the merry-go-round. He silently counted the number of heads that passed him by, preparing to close the gate once the ride had filled to its capacity, because that was his job, but his mind was on that young mother. He looked into the surrounding crowd, but mother and daughter were nowhere to be seen.

That look on the mother's face had struck a chord in him. He had seen that look before, on the face of his own mother. When he was a kid, he had reduced his mother to tears more times than he cared to remember. He wasn't sure what it was about her, but he went through a phase where he wasn't happy unless he was tormenting her. He hated himself for those years. Sure, he blamed her for his father's leaving, but he shouldn't have treated her like that, but he was a kid back then and didn't know any better. Then again, he knew better now, but that didn't stop him.

Shit!

He had lost count, and there were a half dozen people walking around aimlessly in search of an open carousel animal to ride.

Terry raised his hand to stop the line from entering through the open gate. He called to the extra people he had let on the ride. "Sorry about that. You'll be first in line for the next ride."

"Suckers!" laughed the man with the big head, straddling a large white horse.

After his obligatory pass around the ride, making sure all the little kids were strapped in properly, Terry pressed the green button, and the ride began to move, horses and people revolving, bobbing up and down, for the next two-and-a-half minutes.

"I love carousels," a woman said.

Terry turned, hoping it would be someone his age, but to his disappointment, the woman was older, in her thirty's, he figured. She was still cute though, although he didn't go for older women.

"I find them very cool," the woman added. She stood first in line.

Terry smiled. "I'm embarrassed to say it, but when I was a kid, I was afraid of them."

"Like that little girl?" The woman asked.

"I didn't have pigtails," Terry smiled.

"I find them fascinating," the woman said.

"Really? What's so fascinating about a carousel?"

"Lots of things. Did you know that most carousels have a lead horse?"

"No. What's a lead horse?"

"A lead horse stands out from all the rest. It's usually the biggest, most beautifully decorated horse, and they say, that every carousel has one. I'm writing a book about it."

"No kidding?"

"I'm traveling across the country visiting as many amusement parks as I can," the woman said.

"Really? How cool!"

"It's slow-going, though. It gets to be rather expensive."

"Why don't you just do a Google search?" Terry asked.

The woman laughed. "Now you sound like my agent. No, I have to see these things in person. Ride them. A Google search doesn't cut it. This ride here has a lead horse."

"It does?"

"Yep. It's the big one right in front of the chariot. It should be coming around again. Wait, wait—there it is!"

She pointed to the horse in front of the chariot.

"See how it's different from the others?" She asked.

Terry saw that it was larger than the other horses, its body wider, bulkier. Whereas the other horses' heads were all cocked slightly either to the left or to the right, the lead horse looked straight ahead, its eyes blazing. It was indeed beautifully decorated, its green, blue, and red gear more ornate than that of the other horses, its orange coat more plush. Its mouth was open, as if neighing, and it looked like the sort of animal that could easily trample a man, although its expression was anything but threatening. Majestic was the word that came to Terry's mind.

"I've been coming here my whole life, and I've never noticed that," Terry said.

"I doubt anybody notices. That's why I'm writing a book about lead horses. I think people will be interested. I might even include a chapter about why little kids are so afraid of these rides."

"Because they're little kids. They're afraid of everything," Terry said.

"What was it about the horses that frightened you?"

"I wasn't afraid of the horses."

"No? What were you afraid of?"

"I was afraid of the paintings."

Terry pointed upwards

On the panels in the center of the ride were mirrors surrounded by gaudy flashing lights, so the riders could see themselves going up and down. Above each mirror was a painting, each one of a different animal. There were bison, bears, lions, tigers, deer, and even a lobster.

"I was especially frightened of that one," Terry said, pointing upwards once again.

He pointed to a portrait of an elephant dressed in human clothing. It wore a white shirt covered by a red vest and dark blue pants. The beast stood erect in a very human posture, with its front paws on its hips. Its face looked directly outwards, directly into the eyes of all who looked at him. It was scowling and looked hopelessly grumpy.

"He is a rather unpleasant looking fellow," the woman said.

In the background of the painting, large green trees towered over a group of children playing in a meadow. Two of the children held balloons, while the third and smallest child reached skyward as an errant yellow balloon flew towards the sky.

Each painting was similar to this, with an animal in the foreground, and children in the background either in a rural or carnival setting. All brightly colored, they were obviously intended to be cheery, but Terry had always found them unnerving, the same way he had always been uncomfortable around clowns.

"I wonder why he frightened you so much?" the woman asked.

"I don't know," Terry answered. "I think it was the way he looked at me. I didn't like the fact that he always seemed to be staring at me, ready to pounce on me in a fit of anger or something. It bothered me so much I actually had nightmares about it."

"No kidding?"

"It was some pretty freaky shit—oh, sorry."

The woman laughed. "That's okay. I say 'shit' all the time. I do it, too. Three times a day. That too much information for you?"

Terry chuckled. "You're pretty funny."

"I just like to be crude. It's the writer in me."

Terry looked at the green light which suddenly blinked three times.

"Time to stop the ride. Hey, good luck with your book."

"Thanks."

"Too bad I'll never see you again," Terry said. He flinched immediately. It wasn't like him to be so forward, but he had enjoyed the conversation.

"It's a small world," she said.

He pressed the button and the ride began to slow to a halt.

"I'd ask you for your phone number, but you probably wouldn't want to go out with someone as—" he paused, and realized he'd better be careful with what he said next. No mention of "young" or "old." "—as unseasoned as me."

"Unseasoned? What are you? A piece of meat?"

She suddenly burst out laughing. "That didn't come out right."

"That wasn't you being crude?" Terry asked.

"No, I'm afraid I can't take credit for that one. I meant meat on a barbecue, not—you know."

The woman reached into her small purse and scribbled on a piece of paper. "It's my cell. I'm only in town for one more night, but I'd love to see you. And don't worry. When I was talking to you just now, I didn't think I was talking to my kid brother."

"I don't even know your name," Terry said.

"Amy," she said.

"Amy," he smiled, as he opened the gate and let her and the rest of the line onto the merry-go-round for the next ride.

Terry lay on his back on the bed. Amy was next to him, asleep. Her perfume smelled good. He wasn't sure what scent it was, but it was sexy and erotic. It had gotten him excited even before she started kissing him.

It was the first time he had ever slept with someone older than him, and he had definitely liked it. Too bad Amy wasn't sticking around. She was off the next morning to Chicago to continue the research for her book. It was just as well. He wasn't looking for a relationship right now, not before his final year of college.

He looked at Amy sleeping next to him wearing nothing but that sexy perfume. Then again, more time together wouldn't have been a bad thing.

The digital clock by the bed read 1:05. Why was he still awake? Usually he fell right to sleep after sex. Not tonight. For some reason his mind was racing.

Maybe it was the fact that he was in Amy's hotel room and not his own bed at home. It was possible, of course, but he doubted it. He usually slept well wherever the hell he decided to hang his head. If it had been up to Amy, they would have been sleeping in his own bed. When she learned that he was staying at his mom's house for the summer, she had been quick to suggest that they "do it" in the bedroom where he had grown up. She found that terribly sexy. He did too, but he doubted his mother would agree. So, he quickly struck down that idea.

His mind continued to rev like a poorly calibrated engine. He began thinking of the elephant nightmare from his childhood, how he used to wake up in the middle of the night to see the elephant from the carousel picture and a bison standing at the foot of his bed. They'd be on their hind legs, just the way they were in the paintings, and they'd walk towards him, one on each side of his bed. The elephant would say his name, in a voice that was full and gruff. The voice alone, threatening and mean, had been enough to bring him to tears, but there was more. The two animals would reach for him, touch him on the stomach, and then they'd tickle him, tickle him until he cried, and he'd wake up screaming.

The nightmare would always begin the same way. He'd hear the carnival music first, the same tune which was piped through the tinny speakers of the merry-go-round. It was supposed to be cheery music, but to him, it was creepy and haunting. It was music that was filled with dread, and when he heard it, he'd cower and cover his eyes with his blanket, because he knew what he was about to see.

It was pointless to hide. There was no place to go.

He'd uncover his face and he'd look anyway, through his window at the street below, and he'd see a creepy old man standing outside his bedroom window. Just standing there, smiling up at him, partly bent over at the waist, as if he had a kink in his back, or a pain in his side. The man would stand there smiling without saying a word, and he'd watch with animated curiosity as the elephant and bison passed him on either side, walking on their hind legs, towards the bedroom window.

He'd retreat to his bed, and then he would hear the padded footsteps of the elephant and the hard hoof beats of the bison, creeping along the hardwood floor of the hallway leading to his bedroom. Just before they'd enter his room, he'd *smell* them. He would always be painfully aware of the pungent odor of animal.

The smell of animal.

He smelled it now.

He opened his eyes. No light. Darker than dark. Terry sensed immediately the preternatural cover which blanketed the room. His eyes roved back and forth. The darkness suffocated him. No light from outside the window, no red numbers on the digital clock, no green on the coffeemaker.

He sniffed, and the animal odor in the room was unmistakable. He reached over, and his hand fell upon the mattress. Amy was gone.

Like a frightened child, he weakly called out her name. *"Amy?"*

A deep resonating snort answered him, from the snout of an animal.

The bison.

"No fucking way!" he cried.

Despite the darkness, an all too recognizable silhouette appeared at the foot of his bed, the hulking body, the fury mane, the heavy horns. A second figure emerged from the shadows to the left of the hairy beast, a larger and more ominous figure, with a more massive body and a wider header. Even in the black night, Terry made out the trunk.

The animal odor assaulted his nasal passages, momentarily choking him.

The bison closed in on his bed, and stood above him, and Terry gasped as he saw his face for the first time, and it was even more hideous than he remembered. The hair around the beast's head gave the impression that he had a beard, and the horns made Terry think of the devil, but it was the eyes, those wet beads of moisture that seemed to be dripping blood, that got to him, cut through to his soul. Tiny wet eyes, looking down at him with an intense gaze of horror and hatred, as if the creature had waited its entire life to catch up to Terry and to finally harm him. The beast looked ready to pounce, as if Terry had inflicted some awful harm to him in the past and he was there now to seek retribution.

"Please," Terry whispered. "Don't."

The bison snorted, and moisture dribbled down from its snout onto the Terry's naked chest.

"What do you want?" Terry asked.

The bison did not respond. He never did. It was always the elephant who had taken the lead in the torture, in inflicting pain upon him. Why should it be different now after all these years?

A low husky breathing fell upon his face. The elephant. Terry flinched.

The massive animal lowered its head towards Terry's face. The expression on the animal's face was like the bison's full of extreme hatred. Why? Why did they hate him? What had Terry ever done to them?

"We've come back for you. You, a descendant. Your great-grandfather once worked for a circus. He was a carpenter by trade, but he also worked for the circus, and many a year the circus was held on the grounds the amusement park is built upon. His specialty was a cat-o'-nine-tails. When he used it on us, he called it—'tickling.'"

A shriek pierced the air. It was a child.

Terry suddenly heard a bunch of voices, and everything went white. He blinked, and when he opened his eyes, he wasn't in the motel room anymore; he was lying on his back on the floor of the amusement park carousel. The two creatures were still with him, still holding him down. A large hook was plunged into his gut. He gasped. In the light, he could see his stomach covered with blood. He fought back the urge to vomit.

The voices came from the crowd of people standing in line to ride the carousel. He heard the cheesy music pumped through the park speakers, smelled the aroma of freshly popped popcorn and greasy pizza, and he could even hear the roar of the wooden roller coaster in the distance. As best he could tell, he really was at the carousel at the park.

He looked at the people in line. Nobody was coming to his rescue. In fact, no one seemed to notice him. They couldn't see him. Somehow, they couldn't see him, as if he and his torturers were invisible.

He heard a child's cry again, and this time when Terry looked at the line, he spied a little boy, a toddler who couldn't have been any older than three, holding onto his dad's hand, screaming, twisting and turning, fighting to break out of his dad's grip, all the while looking at Terry.

The child could see them.

"He can see us," Terry said. He looked at the other young children in line. They were screaming and crying as well.

"All the kids can see us!"

"They see what they are able to see. They see, and they remember. Remember what will happen to them if they harm our kind. Chained, beaten, our flesh ripped open with hooks. All in the name of training.

Denied food and water! Pushed, shoved, crushed by bulldozers! That is our fate while we walk this earth. We are powerless to fight you, until afterwards, now, when we return as spirits and make you see. Make you feel."

The elephant jammed the hook deep into Terry's gut.

Terry screamed.

He opened his eyes to see Amy looking down upon him curiously.

"W-what?" he asked weakly.

"I'm just looking at you," Amy said. "You were dreaming."

"I was? Yes, I must have been dreaming," he whispered.

He rubbed his eyes and noticed it wasn't dark anymore. It was morning.

"The smell," he muttered.

Amy frowned. "Are you saying I smell?" She sniffed her armpit.

Terry shook his head. "No."

Amy sniffed again. "Of course, we do kind of smell. Like sex. Sorry. Is that a turn-off for you? Do I smell bad?"

"No."

"That's good, because I love the smell of sex. It's so nice and dirty!"

"It was the smell of animal."

Amy nodded. "That's what I'm talking about. Pure animal passion!"

Again, Terry shook his head. "No. Not us. Real animals. I had that dream again, I guess. The one I was telling you about, with the elephant and the bison. It was so real. I thought it was really happening."

"I'm sorry. I didn't realize you had nightmare," Amy said. "You were whimpering in your sleep. You sounded like a little boy, but I didn't think you were frightened."

"I wonder why I had that dream again now after all these years?" Terry asked.

"Who knows why we dream anything? Dreams are freaky," Amy said.

"This was more than a dream. It was real," Terry said.

Amy laughed. "Sure it was."

Terry ignored her. "It was like the ones I had when I was a kid, but this time, there was something more, but fuck me if I can't remember."

"Sure, I will," Amy smiled.

Her words prompted Terry to grin. "No, I was saying that I'm certain this time things were different. Things went in a direction they hadn't before, but for the life of me, I can't remember any of it."

"Too bad. Do you remember these at least?" She played with her boobs.

"Of course I remember those," he said. He took a long gaze at Amy's nakedness and loved what he saw. "You're beautiful."

He reached up and kissed her full on the lips. It was nearly a perfect moment, except that his nostrils were full of animal scent.

Was it just a dream, Terry asked himself? Of course it was. It was all a dream.

But if this were truly true, why was he having such a difficult time believing it? He knew the answer. His memories from his childhood were a hodgepodge of mixed images and emotions. Who could tell what was real and what was imagined?

As an adult, he didn't have this problem. He clearly knew what was a dream and what was real. The experience he had the other night in the motel room with Amy was not a dream. He had seen clearly, distinctly, and with incredible detail the faces of the bison and the elephant. They were in the room with him. That much he knew.

Why Amy hadn't seen them, why when he had opened his eyes the first time Amy had been missing from the bed and there had been such an incredible veil of darkness enveloping the room, he did not know. He couldn't make sense of any of it. But he knew it wasn't a dream.

This scared the shit out of him.

Had he been a child, he wouldn't have known and he would have simply called it a nightmare. But he was not a child. He was an adult, and he knew that on some level he had been visited by those carousel animals.

What did it all mean?

He didn't know.

But he understood.

Understood that there were things that children saw that couldn't be chalked up to just bad dreams. He understood this because he had seen one of these things with his own eyes. He just couldn't remember what it was.

Terry pressed the red button and the ride came to a slow halt. As he let the riders off the ride, a man holding his young son wiped the tears from the child's eyes.

"There, you see? I told you there was nothing to be afraid of. Wasn't that fun?"

The little boy nodded, tentatively.

The man looked at Terry. "Can you imagine being afraid of a carousel?"

Terry's insides throbbed. His stomach was sore, and he felt as if he'd spent the night throwing up with the dry heaves. Animal scent filled his nostrils

Terry smiled at the man but didn't answer, because he knew what it was like to be afraid of these rides.

Terry looked at the little boy, and for a moment, the child looked familiar, and he understood that the child's fear was based on something real. What specifically this little boy was afraid of he couldn't know for sure, but he felt in his gut that he had a pretty good idea of what it was. There was something about the carousel and fear, something that little children saw when they came here, something they took back with them when they went home at night to sleep, something about—the animals.

I love westerns. Better yet, I love that rare hybrid of western and horror, which is why I wrote this story.

THE BLUFF

When Sheriff Richard Malloy stepped onto the dusty main street of Kilmer City, his steady hand inches above his right holster, and faced down the nameless stranger who had ridden into town the night before, he was alone. The townsfolk were all there, hidden, peeking from behind drawn curtains and barricaded windows, but they weren't there for their sheriff. If they wanted to see anything, it was the sight of the nameless stranger gunning down their lawman in cold blood.

Sheriff Malloy was well aware of where his town stood. For some men, this would have been enough to crush their spirits, but not Malloy. He relished the moment and looked forward to telling the cowards afterwards, *"I'm still here."*

The nameless stranger with the grizzled face and cigarette butt hanging from his clenched lips was fast, really fast. In fact, there was no doubt in Malloy's mind that this gunslinger would beat him to the draw.

Even better.

"What are you waiting for?" Malloy asked. "I told you to get out of my town."

The stranger removed the butt from his lips and spit onto the ground. "I kinda like it here. A guy could get real comfortable in a town like this. It has all the amenities. I think I'll stay. Of course, if you don't like my stayin, you're welcome to climb on that horse behind you and ride your ass out of here."

Malloy said nothing. There was nothing else to say. It was time.

He stared long and hard into the stranger's eyes, and both men knew exactly what was going to happen next.

Malloy reached for his gun, but the stranger beat him to it and blasted a hole in his chest right through his heart. The impact knocked the sheriff back several steps, but he didn't go down. Instead, he grabbed his gun, aimed, and pulled the trigger. The bullet shattered the stranger's forehead right between his eyes, and the shocked gunman's legs buckled, and he collapsed in a heap of dust, dead.

Malloy turned towards the windows of the tavern where he knew the men of Kilmer City had gathered, and smiled.

Doc Miller found the mayor behind his desk, Tom Huddleston with his back to him looking out the window, and Henry Beauchamp sitting in the large seat opposite the mayor's desk, with his right leg crossed over his left knee, looking as relaxed as ever, but the doc knew better. None of them were relaxed these days.

"Come on in, doctor. I trust you were discreet," the mayor said.

"Of course."

"Are you sure he didn't see you?" Tom asked, as he turned from the window.

"Well, I didn't see him, so I'm assuming he didn't see me," Miller answered.

"He sees everything. He knows we're here!" Tom said, his voice full of panic.

"Stop it," Henry Beauchamp said from his chair. "We have to hold ourselves together or else we're not going to accomplish anything. Things around here are tense enough as it is. We don't need to be making things worse by getting all worrisome."

"Aren't you worried?" Tom asked.

"Of course I am, who wouldn't be?" Henry answered. "But we've got to keep ourselves together and come up with a solution to this problem. Fast."

"Henry's right," the mayor agreed. "We need to come up with a solution."

"What solution?" Tom asked. "We've hired three gunslingers, he's killed them all! Two of them actually shot him, yet he survived! How do we deal with that?"

"Yes, doc, what about that?" Henry asked. "I saw him take a bullet straight to the heart, we all saw it, yet he never went down. Hell, he hardly moved. He just stood there, took the bullet, and gunned down our hired man. Yet, he still saw you afterwards. What happened inside your office?"

The doctor cleared his throat. "Well, he asked me to remove the bullet. What was I going to do, say no? Like the rest of you, I'd like to live to see tomorrow!"

"But how is he not dead?" Henry asked.

"He's not dead because—in my opinion, he's no longer human."

"Not human? Jesus Christ, what the hell are you talking about, doc?" Tom asked.

"Richard Malloy, our sheriff, is no longer human. He's inhuman. He's superhuman."

"In plain English, doc, what does that mean?" Henry asked.

"It means, I removed a bullet from his heart without so much as a drop of whiskey in him and he didn't flinch, didn't feel a thing! Within moments, the scar healed. He said he just wanted the bullet out to avoid infection. I don't know what's happened to our sheriff, but I do know one thing. It's not an act of God. More likely, it's the work of the devil."

"No shit, doc!" Tom said. "He's killing people in town left and right, he's raping our women, he looks like a walking corpse, and he can't be killed! I'd say he sounds like the devil!"

"Are you saying the devil has come to Kilmer City?" Henry asked.

"If not the devil, something evil. A demon, perhaps?" the doctor said.

"Anyway, gentlemen, we're wasting time. The question remains, what are we going to do about him?" the mayor asked. "I for one am fresh out of ideas, except for fleeing this town like a jack rabbit out of a wolf's den."

"We can't flee, remember? That's what Paul Sysko did, and look what happened to him? Malloy caught him at the edge of town and stuck a spear through his chest like a pig on a spit," Tom said. "We're stuck here, and unless we come up with a plan, we're all gonna die!"

"I'd offer him a couple of thousand dollars if I thought he could be bought," Henry said. "But he'd probably kill me just for making the suggestion."

"What about a specialist in evil?" the mayor suggested.

"We did that already. The eminent Professor Artemis Caruthers," Henry said, recalling the name. "With all those letters after his name from those fine east coast institutions of higher learning. I had a lot of faith in Professor Caruthers. All that talk he gave us about being an expert in demonology. I thought Malloy was a goner. How did you say Caruthers died again?"

"You don't want to know," the doctor said, shaking his head. "But it had something to do with the removal of all his internal organs."

"What about a priest or a minister?" the mayor asked.

"Like Reverend Dobe?" Tom asked. "A mighty fine religious man, the good reverend. He served us well for many years. Until Malloy showed up. Now Dobe's dead!"

"What about one of those Catholics?" Henry asked.

"That's a possibility," the doctor agreed.

"I have an idea, but I wasn't going to mention it because it's far-fetched. I don't know. You gentlemen will never go for it," Tom said.

"Let us be the judge of that. If you have an idea, spit it out, son," Henry said.

"About a month ago, on one of my business trips, I came upon this man in a saloon, a gambler, a real slick fellow, but not the weasel type. This guy could back himself up with his fists. I saw it with my own eyes, after he had won a hand in poker, and the loser didn't take to kindly to losing. He leapt at my guy, and he struck down the loser with two quick blows to the throat," Tom said.

"That's not going to help us. Malloy survives bullets to the heart. A blow to the throat's not going to do him no harm," Henry said.

"Let me finish. It was something this guy said, that stayed with me," Tom continued. "He said, 'I can bluff the devil.' That's how he won so much at cards. I was there a while and watched him. Game after game, situation after situation, it was impossible to know what he was thinking. A man like that, Malloy's not going to be able to read so carefully, and there's more. We got to talking, him and I. He told me his name was Clay Gannon."

"Gannon? The con man?" Henry asked.

"You know him?" Tom said.

"Who's Clay Gannon?" the doctor asked.

"Only the biggest con artist this side of the Mississippi," Henry said. "And this is your idea, Tom? To hire Clay Gannon? What's he going to do? Con Malloy to death?"

"See, I knew I shouldn't have suggested it," Tom said.

"What exactly would this Clay Gannon be able to do for us?" the mayor asked.

"Well, everyone we've hired has failed because Malloy has known exactly what they're doing here and what they're all about," Tom said. "Even the good professor came with a reputation, but Gannon's different. He won't come to town as Clay Gannon. He'll have a plan in place. He'll study the situation and come up with a way to get rid of Malloy that Malloy won't see coming."

"This isn't a con game. Why would Gannon agree to help us?" Henry asked.

"Because you're going to pay him $10,000!"

"Are you out of your mind?" Henry said.

"That was his price. For $10,000 he'd con the devil, that's what he said. He also said he'd do anything for money, and I believe him," Tom said.

"Did you happen to mention he'd be facing off against a demon from hell? A man's not going to do that for money, no matter how high the reward. A dead man can't spend even a dollar, let alone ten thousand!" Henry said.

"But if you had met him, you'd know what I'm talking about," Tom said. "He's just crazy enough. What would it hurt to ask him?'

"It wouldn't," the mayor said. "Hire him."

Clay Gannon sat in a chair by the edge of the hotel bed and smiled at his guests, the mayor, the doc, Henry Beauchamp, one of the richest landowners and cattle men around, and the man who was going to pay his salary for this job, and Tom Huddleston, the young businessman who had hired him. He liked Huddleston. He seemed more honest than most up-and-coming businessmen his age. In his line of work, he had to be amazingly good at reading people, and he was, and every indication told him Tom Huddleston was a man he could trust.

"I thought I had heard everything," Gannon said, "but a demon sheriff. I have to admit, that one I hadn't heard!"

Gannon, a handsome figure with an athletic build and an amiable face, with short black hair without a trace of gray that made him look no older than thirty, gave out a chuckle. No one else laughed.

"Am I to understand correctly, that you agree to our terms, that you'll 'take care of' Richard Malloy for $10,000?" Henry asked.

"Yes, and no," Gannon said. "I actually came into town two days ago, under the guise of a traveling salesman, to avoid any suspicion from your sheriff. I've had some time to look around, to take in the sights, to gather the feel, sounds, and smells of your town. In short, to clear my head to come up with a game plan."

"Have you? Come up with a game plan?" Tom asked.

"Yes, but it'll cost you more than $10,000."

"Do you realize how much money that is?" Henry asked.

"Keep your shirt on, Beauchamp. I don't want any more money. But I do want something else from you."

"What?"

"Your daughter, Mel, is right beautiful. What is she, nineteen? Throw her into the deal, and I'll dispose of your demon sheriff."

"You son of a bitch! You can go to hell!" Henry said.

"From what you folks have described, I'd say I'm already here," Gannon smiled. "Yes, gentlemen, I'm asking for a lot, but then again, so are you. I may not live to collect my fee, so Beauchamp, the odds say that you'll get to keep your money and your daughter."

"That is a highly irregular request, sir," the mayor said. "We're not in the habit of making such off color business dealings. It's perverted!"

"You're not in the habit of making such business dealings? Well, I am," Gannon said. "And as far as it being perverted, the girl is of age, isn't she? Then, there's nothing perverted about it. Fathers have been arranging marriages for their daughters for generations."

"Marriage? You want to marry her?" Henry asked.

"Forgive me, I misspoke. I don't want to marry your daughter. I just want to spend one night in the sack with her, and suck on those nice titties of hers."

"You son of a bitch!" Henry shouted, and Tom and the doctor had to restrain him.

"It's a good deal, if you think about it," Gannon said. "She just has to give me one night, one night of irrepressible lovemaking, and then she's free to leave and go on with the rest of her life. Besides, if you haven't noticed, Beauchamp, I'm a right good looking fella. It could be one of the best nights of your daughter's life. Hell, she might even thank you afterwards."

"You bastard! To hell with you!" Henry roared.

"What if we make it $11,000, instead?" the mayor suggested.

"No. I want the girl. You see, in a situation like this, it's going to be really tough, and I just might find myself in a bind where I'm going to have to reach back and reach for something extra, and the knowledge that a night in bed with that beautiful naked supple teen body might be just the ticket to get me over the hump and deliver to you that demon sheriff you're so desperate to get rid of. Think about it. I already have. I have a plan in place, and it will succeed."

"What's your plan?" Tom asked.

"Can't tell you. You know that. From what you've said, your sheriff always seems to know what's going on ahead of time. It's better that the only one in town who knows is me. By the way, I want the terms of our deal in writing. That way, when I get rid of the bastard, I'm guaranteed my reward. You'll give me the terms of the deal in writing?"

"Yes," the mayor said.

"Then we have a deal?" Gannon asked. "If I were you, Beauchamp, I wouldn't worry. It's clear to everyone in this room that the odds favor your sheriff."

"If we didn't need to get rid of him so badly—" Henry said.

"But you do need to get rid of him so badly, and that's why I'm holding all the cards," Gannon smiled. "Do we have a deal, gentlemen?"

"Henry, it's up to you," the mayor said.

"God, forgive me," Henry said.

"I guess they weren't kidding when they said you were possessed by the devil," Gannon said.

Sheriff Malloy, as pale as a corpse, glared at him with eyes that seemed to glow red.

"You look like shit, and this whole place is as cold as a cave," Gannon said. He had been surprised at how frigid the sheriff's office had seemed when he had entered the room. So cold he half expected to see icicles hanging from the ceiling. Yet, it was a different kind of cold than winter. It had the feeling of evil about it.

"You spend much time in caves, Mr. Gannon?" Malloy asked.

"I've been in one or two in my day. It's a good place to take a girl. Well, every man has his peculiarities. I can tell you have a few."

"What do you know about me?" Malloy asked.

"Just what the townsfolk told me, which isn't much. They think you're the devil. What exactly did happen to you? You weren't always like this. You used to be a respectable law man."

"You know, you're the first person to ask me that question since this all happened to me," Malloy said.

"That's because I'm the first person who's come within talking distance of you who you haven't killed!"

"That's because you haven't pulled a gun on me or tried to sprinkle me with holy water."

"So, what happened?" Gannon asked.

"I made a deal and lost."

"Isn't that always the way?"

"Remember Rick Dunbarton and the Grissam Gang?"

"Sure do. They were the meanest cattle thieves in the land, until you shot Rick dead and brought in the rest of the gang to justice."

"I could never have done that on my own. So I made a deal with this man I knew, a self-proclaimed demonologist. He told me if I sold my soul, Dunbarton's bullets wouldn't affect me. I didn't really believe him, but for me, it was like having a lucky rabbit's foot. I figured, why not? I needed all the help I could get. So I made the deal. Dunbarton's bullet hit me in the right shoulder, but I didn't go down. That's how I was able to shoot that bastard dead. But a week later, the demon I sold my soul to came to collect."

"What? A red devil with horns, tail, and a pitchfork showed up at your door?" Gannon chuckled.

"No. I woke up one morning, and he was inside me. You know how I knew? I strangled my dog." Malloy looked away. "I loved that old dog."

"This demon, does he have a name?" Gannon asked.

"Yeah. Yeah he has a name. His name is Fuck You."

"A Chinese demon, I see," Gannon said.

Malloy ignored the jest. "He's inside me. Right now he's in here." Malloy thumped his chest. "He's the one running the show. And when he takes over, those close to me—die. Just letting you know, in case you have any misconceptions about leaving here alive."

"So, that's your master plan? To kill everyone around you until there's no one left?" Gannon asked.

"I don't know what his master plan is, except that he wants to live," Malloy said. "Which is why you have to die, because you've come here to kill me."

"No, I haven't."

"Really? That's news to me."

"Well, that's what I told the folks who hired me, and that's what you've heard people around town saying, but it's not true," Gannon said.

"Why are you here, then?"

"Officially, Henry Beauchamp is paying me $10,000 to do you in, and I asked him to throw in his daughter Mel for good measure, just for one night. Well, truth be told, I'm a rich man. I don't really want his money, but I do want the girl, and for more than one night. Remember those peculiarities I was talking about? Well, I have a lot of those, and what I have in store for young Mel isn't something that her daddy is going to like, which is where you come in."

"Me?"

"All I want is the girl, and under the present arrangement, after I'm through with her, she goes back to her daddy, and once Henry Beauchamp learns what I did with her, he's going to come after me with a posse seeking my head in a noose. I can't have that. So, here's the deal: I don't kill you. You let me walk out of here. I get the girl. You take care of Henry Beauchamp for me, and you can take his $10,000. Hell, after he's dead you can take all his goddamn money. Look, I just want the girl. This was never about killing you. It was my way of getting insurance so I can have the girl, you take care of Beauchamp for me, and you get all his money to boot. How's that for a deal?"

"You'd walk away from $10,000 for one night with a girl?"

"I love money, but I'm addicted to women," Gannon said. "Besides, I can make the $10,000 back easy. That's what poker is for. How do you think I've earned all my money in the first place? What do you say?"

"You must take me for a fool, Mr. Gannon. I know who you are. You're a con man. I don't trust you," Malloy said.

"That's too bad, because think of all the things you and your demon friend inside of you could do with all of Beauchamp's money."

"I don't need you to get Beauchamp's money. It's there for the taking whenever I want it."

"Okay. So, how can I sweeten the deal? If it's not money you want, what is it, then?" Gannon asked. "Look, you just threatened to kill me. I'm dealing for my life here. I'm all in. What do you want?"

"Souls," Malloy answered. "In this case, your soul. Sell your soul to me, Mr. Gannon. Then we might have a deal."

"Let me get this straight. I sell my soul to you, and in return I get Beauchamp's daughter?"

Malloy nodded.

"That's a hefty price," Gannon said.

"Think of the alternative."

"There is that. So, how does one go about selling one's soul, exactly? What is it I have to do?" Gannon asked.

"Just give me your word and it's a done deal. It's as simple as that," Malloy said.

"That's it? You mean, I don't have to sign my name in blood or anything like that?"

"No."

A moment passed without either man uttering a word.

"What's it going to be, Gannon?" Malloy asked. "Sell your soul and get the girl, or die?"

"There's a third option you've overlooked," Gannon said.

"What's that?"

"You let me leave, and we forget this meeting ever took place."

"Fat chance of that happening," Malloy barked.

"Then, of course, there's my original offer," Gannon said, "which I still think is a mighty fine deal."

"For you, maybe. You get the girl and your life. What do I get? Beauchamp's life and his money, two things I already have, if I care to take them. No, sell me your soul, or I end your existence right here, right now."

"How soon would it happen?" Gannon asked. "If I agree, and I give you my word, how much longer would I have to be myself?"

"Long enough for you to enjoy some of those peculiarities you were talking about with Beauchamp's daughter."

Gannon didn't respond. The two men stared into each other's eyes, locking their gazes as if they were preparing to draw their weapons.

"As I said, selling my soul is a hefty price. Too hefty a price if you ask me. Surely, there must be some other way."

Malloy paused, as if he were still sizing Gannon up.

"There is," the sheriff finally said. "You could offer a sacrifice. To me."

"What sort of sacrifice are we—"

"The girl," Malloy said. He grinned. "Sacrifice the girl to me, give up what you want most, and I'll let you live. I'll grant you your life, but not your freedom."

"Come again?" Gannon asked.

"Afterwards, you'll work for me."

"Work for you? Doing what?"

"Whatever I say. I could use a man with your talents."

"For how long?"

"Until I have no further need of you."

"Do I get to spend time with the girl beforehand, at least?"

"No."

"So, why should I—"

"There are other women."

"This doesn't sound like a very good deal for me."

"It gives you your life."

"Yes, well, I suppose it does. So, if I agree to this, you won't kill me?"

"Not today," Malloy grinned.

"Live to see tomorrow, that's what I always say," Gannon smiled. "All right, sheriff, you have yourself a deal. Shall we shake on it?"

Gannon extended his hand. Malloy did not reciprocate.

"No," Malloy said.

Mel opened her eyes. Everything was a blur. She had gone to bed, fallen asleep as always, but then she had heard a noise in her dream, like glass breaking. She thought she had opened her eyes to see a man in her room, but that's the last thing she remembered, until now.

She was in a bed. She was freezing. To her horror and embarrassment, she was completely naked.

"Evening," Sheriff Malloy said.

Mel opened her mouth to scream, but nothing came out.

"It's no use. You cannot scream," Malloy said. "You are drugged. I injected you with a muscle relaxant and sedative. Not only have you lost the ability to move your arms and legs, but your tongue and throat muscles are also useless. You cannot make a sound. I'm surprised you can even open your mouth. You also won't be able to feel pain. Which is a good thing."

Gannon stepped from the shadows.

"What do I need to do?" Gannon whispered to Malloy. He appeared uncomfortable with the situation. "Plunge a—a knife into her heart?"

Mel's eyes widened.

"Nothing so simple-minded," Malloy answered. "For you to earn my trust and live, you'll need to do something more. You're going to dismember her. Alive."

Gannon chose to offer no reaction, although he allowed himself to swallow and let his natural abhorrence to the idea gradually show.

Malloy turned to Mel, who lay helplessly still on the bed. "That's right, darling. We're going to dismember you. Cut off your arms and legs, one limb at a time."

Mel tried to squirm and fight, but she couldn't move a muscle. Her eyes widened ever so slightly in horror and panic.

Malloy lifted a hacksaw from a tray behind him. He handed it to Gannon.

"Start with her left arm," Malloy said.

"Don't you want to say something first?" Gannon asked. "Some sort of invocation or demonic prayer or something?"

"No. Her left arm. *Now.*"

Gannon placed the hacksaw down on the bed and rubbed his hands on his pants.

"Sweaty palms," Gannon said. "I need to dry them off."

He reached into his right pocket and removed a cloth which he used to wipe his hands further.

"I didn't take you for a nervous, man, Gannon."

"Usually, I'm not, but it's not every day I'm asked to sever a woman's arms and legs from her body."

"I'm pleased that I was able to impress you."

"I didn't say I was impressed," Gannon said. "I'm just—uncomfortable."

"Then I'm pleased I was able to make you feel uncomfortable."

"Let's get this over with," Gannon said. He put the cloth back into his pocket and grabbed the hacksaw.

"Left arm first, you said?"

Malloy nodded.

Gannon stepped to the right side of the bed and with his free hand took hold of the girl's left arm. He looked into the girl's eyes and saw nothing. He knew she had to be terrified, but her face was still. Even her eyes didn't move. He smelled body odor and saw streams of sweat oozing from her left armpit. He looked over her naked body and saw that it was covered in beads of sweat.

Gannon pressed the saw down hard against her flesh and broke her skin, drawing blood. He allowed his own body to tremble.

"What are you waiting for, Gannon? Do it!" Malloy ordered.

Once again, Gannon placed the saw down on the bed, and he again retrieved a cloth from his pocket, this one from his left pocket, but instead of wiping his hands, he wiped the saw handle.

"It was covered in my sweat, I'm sorry. I couldn't get a good grip," Gannon said. He put the cloth back inside his left pocket. "I'm—feeling light-headed—I can't—Could you—just—start slicing, and I'll finish. Just make the initial cut, and I'll take it from there. Please."

"You're pathetic," Malloy said. "Give me the damn saw."

Gannon shook his head. "I'm going to be sick." He keeled over and started retching in the corner.

Malloy huffed. "Fucking pussy."

He took the saw, gripped it firmly and placed it down hard on Mel's arm.

"Look here, Gannon, you shit-for-brains coward. I'm going to cut her down to the bone, and you're going to take over from there. If you don't, I'll gut you like a pig right here, but not before I make you watch me—"

Malloy stopped talking. He grimaced in pain.

"What the fuck?"

He felt his head swoon.

"What did you—" He dropped the saw to the ground. "What's happening?"

Gannon kicked the saw away from Malloy.

"You're not the only one with access to powerful drugs,"

Gannon said. "I slipped you a poison, which I wiped onto the handle of the saw."

"I'm a demon. Poisons can't harm me."

"No, but they can kill your body, and without a body, a demon is useless."

"I can repair this body. I am immortal."

Malloy fell to his knees.

"Yeah, well, good luck with that," Gannon said. "See, this poison acts like an acid. It eats away at your internal organs, obliterating them within seconds. In fact, I'd say your heart will be destroyed in just about two seconds from now."

"Impossible. I can read minds."

Gannon smiled. "And you read everything I wanted you to read in mine."

Malloy collapsed face first to the floor, dead.

Gannon jumped towards Mel.

"I'm so sorry I had to put you through this, but if he thought even for a second that I—"

Gannon stopped. He put his ear to Mel's mouth and nose. Not even the faintest breath. Was the girl dead? Or was it the drug? He touched her wrist. No pulse. He swiped the hand-held mirror from the dresser and held it to her mouth and nose. Nothing.

"Christ," he said aloud. "I'm sorry."

He gently closed her eyelids.

"I didn't mean for this to happen to you," he said to her. "I wasn't even going to spend a night with you. That was just part of the bluff. You would have been free to go home to your father. I wouldn't have laid a hand on you. But if I had played things differently, you wouldn't have had a father to go home to."

He kissed her on the forehead, got up and left the room.

He exited the building and headed down the dusty road to deliver the news to his employers and collect his money.

"Darkness" appeared in THE ETERNAL NIGHT CHRONICLE—http://www.eternalnight.co.uk—in 2003 after winning first prize in in THE ETERNAL NIGHT FICTION contest. This long short story/novella was obviously influenced by my divorce, which occurred while I was writing this story.

DARKNESS

It's like this.

We believe we are in control of our lives. From marital status to jobs to lifestyle, we think we're the boss, and even though deep down inside we know in our hearts that life is really just a random series of events where anything can happen, we still cling to this belief that we are at the helm, able to steer our lives in the direction of our choosing.

Therein lies life's comfort zone, the false belief that we are in control. When this belief is shattered, we stumble and fall, like a drunk in a darkened unfamiliar room.

Three days ago I was standing in the supermarket check-out aisle thinking about my wife, Catherine. I'd been stumbling in that darkened room lately, and Cath was the reason why.

"This isn't the life I want, Dylan," she had said out of nowhere. "I can't keep doing the same thing repeatedly. I want something more. I'm no longer in love with you. I'm leaving."

Wow.

And as quickly as she had said it, she had done it, without shedding a tear. She moved out of the house to an apartment, leaving me and our two sons, Sean and Anthony.

Sean's eight and in the third grade, and Anthony is four and in preschool. People, especially men, look at me funny when they hear I'm still a stay at home dad even though the boys are in school. My only answer is, unless you've stayed at home with your children, you don't realize how much kids really need a parent at home, and it's because the little critters demand so much energy, mentally, emotionally, and physically, there has to be someone at home who's full-time job it is to meet their needs.

It was nice to have had this luxury, but now, it's welcome to the real world! I keep hoping Cath will come to her senses and return home before I find a job.

Yes, I want Cath back, because I still love her, despite her leaving, despite the fact that she hurt Sean and Anthony in a way that just wasn't fair for an eight-year-old and a four-year-old. The day I had to witness their crushed faces as she told them she was leaving, that she didn't want to live with daddy anymore, was a day my emotions reached depths of darkness I didn't know existed.

As a man, I had never cried. The night Catherine left, the night I had seen my children scream and shriek as she drove away, I cried—until my eyes had swelled up to the point where I looked like Rocky Balboa.

So there I was in the check-out line thinking pretty much these same thoughts when a bright flash of light shot through the supermarket windows, so bright it caused a collective gasp from the multitude of shoppers.

"Was that lightning?" someone said.

I looked towards the huge glass storefront windows, looking through both the glass and the thin paper signs advertising this week's sales which were taped to the windows. I saw three more flashes in quick succession, none of which were as bright as the first.

"What the hell?" said a large man standing behind me holding a gallon of milk in each hand.

People started moving around, nervously, migrating towards the front of the store. All of a sudden there was lots of chatter, and I could hear in their tone fear, the way people sound after they've just witnessed a car accident. At the same time, the distant rumblings of what sounded like thunder could be heard from outside.

"It can't be thunder," said a man who had apparently only entered the store moments before. "There's not a cloud in the sky!"

"Only in New England," someone else said.

The rumbling grew louder, like a jet plane flying low overhead. The floor beneath my feet began to vibrate, and as I looked around, I could see the food items on the shelves trembling. I thought "earthquake." The experts had been predicting for years that New England was due for a big one.

The rumbling had become a deafening roar, and many people covered their ears.

Those standing by the windows looked up searchingly.

"What do you see out there?" the man with the milk jugs asked.

"It's like a strobe light," said the store manager, having to raise his voice to be heard. He had quickly scurried to the front of his store. He, like everyone else who was by the windows looking up at the sky, held his arms in front of his face, using his hands to shield his eyes. At that point my thoughts went from "earthquake" to "nuclear explosion."

The entire building shook. In the aisle directly behind me, cereal boxes fell from the shelves in an avalanche of colorful cardboard. People started screaming. I saw six or seven frightened shoppers running towards the exit.

Then, a series of violent flashes riddled the outside, and I swear it looked like we were being fired upon. The entire supermarket was engulfed with such a collective gasp I almost fell over. The crowd by the front windows went down, some dropping into crouches while others fell to their hands and knees they were so scared. I covered my eyes with my arm.

Then quiet.

I unshielded my eyes to see the store manager and the others around him slowly returning to their feet. Outside the storefront window, it grew dim, as if a large cloud had passed in front of the sun. This cloudy day sensation lasted but a few seconds before everything out there went pitch black.

It was 2:00 in the afternoon.

"There's no eclipse today," said the man behind me, his voice as dark as the outside.

He had fallen on his butt yet still clung to the two plastic gallons of milk. I offered him my hand, but he shook me off and stood on his own.

"I'm okay," he said.

Slowly, as if in a daze, people began to congregate at the store's exit. Leaving my cart of groceries, that's where I headed as well.

The automatic door swung open, and a young couple raced inside. The manager bounded in front of the crowd.

"What happened out there?" he asked them.

"It was horrible!" the woman cried. She and the man were dressed identically, both in green tops, tan shorts, and sandals.

"It was like someone set a bomb off in the sky!" the man shrieked.

"Alright, take it easy. Calm down," the manager said, and there was an edge to his voice. He knew that that kind of talk was all people needed to hear to turn this dazed quiet crowd into a stampeding frightened mob.

"Now, what exactly did you see?" the manager asked.

The man and woman answered at the same time, their panicked voices canceling each other out. I couldn't make out anything other than the choice words "flashes" and "explosions." Again, that was all people needed to hear.

I felt a sharp pain in my back. A heavyset man with curly hair and glasses, and smelling of b.o., shoved me in the back as he tore his way towards the exit, and I nearly fell over.

"Why don't you watch where the hell you're going!" The man with the milk jugs yelled on my behalf. "You okay?" he asked me.

"Yeah, thanks."

A bunch of people had the same idea as the heavyset man, and they started pushing their way towards the door. A thin woman who looked to be in her sixty's was knocked to the ground.

"Hey! Take it easy!" the manager shouted as he moved to assist the fallen woman. "People are going to get hurt!"

"Shut up and let us leave the store!" someone shouted.

A loud shrill whistle suddenly pierced our eardrums and

more importantly, froze all the fleers in their tracks.

An elderly man wearing a Red Sox cap and standing by the exit removed his fingers from his mouth and smiled.

"That's better," he said. "Listen up. I was out there in the parking lot. I saw the whole thing."

He spoke with a detached calmness that was completely New England.

"What did you see?" my milk jug friend asked.

"One minute the sun was shining, the next there was this flash right where the sun had been, and when I looked up, I saw—the sun looked like it had tripled in size—and then there was this deafening roar, like a jet plane, and a bunch of smaller flashes, and then it was gone."

"What was gone?" the store manager asked.

The old man in the Red Sox cap looked us over carefully, making eye contact with as many of us as possible, as if sizing us up, trying to gauge whether or not we were ready for whatever it was he had to say.

"The sun was gone," he said. "The sun is gone."

"What do you mean, the sun's gone?" someone asked.

"I mean it's not there anymore. Look for yourselves. It's the middle of the day but it's as dark as night."

You could feel the clamor beginning, as if there was going to be this huge collective cry followed by a mad stampede through the exit.

The manager stepped into harm's way, right in front of the exit.

"All right, listen! You all want to get out of here, I know! That's fine, but could you walk out, please? If not, someone's going to get crushed. So use some common sense, okay? Walk. Out. The door! Okay?"

He stepped aside. I looked at the man with the milk jugs.

"You got a family?" he asked.

"Yeah."

"Me, too. Let's get the hell out of here."

I can't speak for the entire crowd, but by the time my milk jug pal and I had made it through, no one had experienced anything worse than a mild push.

Speeding back to Barlow Village in the family minivan, I had the radio on.

"We're trying to get word from the White House to learn just when they'll be making a statement, but it's extremely difficult at this point since these events have only just happened—There was one big flash followed by a bunch of smaller flashes—Witnesses have called ABC News from all across the country. This is something that is affecting the entire nation, and as we are beginning to learn from the various reports coming in, the whole world as well."

As I pulled into our driveway, it was just before 3:00 on this July afternoon. It was as dark as midnight. The lights were on inside the house, and I was glad to see the power hadn't gone out.

Sean and Anthony were at home with our sixteen-year-old babysitter Lara. She needed extra money for the summer, and so a couple of days a week she'd come over to watch the kids while I went food shopping, ran errands, visited the dentist, what have you.

I noticed the temperature had dropped as soon as I had stepped from the van. It couldn't have been warmer than 60 degrees Fahrenheit.

The front screen door swung open, and little Anthony came tearing down the porch stairs. His arms outstretched for balance, he looked like a duck getting ready to fly.

"Daddy! Daddy!"

"Dad!" called my oldest son Sean. He leapt over the porch steps and quickly passed his brother, reaching me first. "We were outside playing, and there was this big flash!" Sean opened his arms to indicate the enormity of the flash.

"Yeah, a big flash!" Anthony added, copying the same gesture his older brother had just made.

"We looked up, and it was like it was all crazy up there!" Sean exclaimed.

"Yeah, all crazy!" Anthony said.

"What do you mean, crazy? What did you see?" I asked, still craving to know what had happened.

"Well, it looked like fireworks only without the colors. It looked like the sun blew up," Sean said. "But that's impossible, isn't it, dad?"

"Yeah," I said right way, though of course I didn't know.

"Are we going to die?" Sean asked suddenly.

"Why do you ask that?"

"Because if the sun *did* blow up, and it's gone now, we can't live, right? We can't live without sunlight, right?"

"I don't want to die!" Anthony said nervously.

"No one's going to die," I assured. As a child, I hated being lied to more than anything else, so as a parent, I made a point to tell the truth to my children. Always. "But you're right, Sean. We can't live without the sun."

Sean looked like he was about to cry. I quickly added, "But we don't know yet if the sun is really gone, now do we?"

"But I saw—"

"We don't know what you saw. Let's just wait and find out. Anyway, I'm home now. Let's get inside. It's cold out here."

As we walked onto the porch, Sean informed me that Lara had been trying to call her mom but the phone wasn't working.

Lara opened the front door and let us inside.

"Thanks, Lara. Are you okay?" I asked.

"Yes," she nodded.

"Sean tells me you've been trying to call your mom?"

"Yeah." Her voice was barely audible. I could tell she was nervous as hell.

"No luck?"

She shook her head.

I walked towards the phone, picked up the cordless and punched "on." Nothing. No sound whatsoever.

"The phone's not working?" Sean asked, again, looking as if he were about to cry.

"No," I said calmly, and I placed the cordless back in its base.

"I miss mommy," Anthony whined. "Is mommy coming home?"

"Boy, isn't that the million dollar question!" I thought. I knelt down to be at eye level with Anthony.

"Mommy's at work at the hospital," I said. "I bet there's lots of accidents today. Mommy's going to be busy for a while."

"What about later? Will she come home later?" Sean asked.

I could taste the bitterness in my mouth like a spoonful of cough medicine.

"I don't know," I said, because I didn't.

"I want mommy," Anthony whined louder.

"I know you do," I whispered. "We'll get together with mommy soon."

"When?" the little guy pressed.

"I don't know. I think we need to bring Lara home, first, and then we can think about getting together with mommy."

"Oh!" Anthony whined yet again. "I want Lara to stay!"

"Me, too!" Sean joined in. "Can't you stay?"

The girl smiled. The boys adored her, and she knew it.

"I think on a day like today, Lara should be with her family," I said.

"We're family!" Sean said.

"Well, we're like family," I clarified, though I didn't know why. Sean was just being difficult on purpose. I turned to Lara. "Do you think your mom's home?"

"Yeah," she said

Just then we heard barking from the backyard. It was our dog, Scout.

"Excuse me," I said. I walked across the house to the back door. "Come on in, Scout."

I opened the door, and in jumped our family pooch, a fifty pound very energetic Dalmatian named Scout. He leapt up at me and licked my face.

"Good to see you, too!" I said, helping him back down on all fours and petting his back.

Scout was nine going on four. He still possessed tremendous vitality for an older dog. It had been Cath's idea way back when to get a dog. Cath had always been a "dog person," and before we were married she was always the one to bond with other people's dogs, but she never quite caught on with Scout. For some reason he bonded more with me.

I remembered something Cath had said just before she left. "I don't like the way I am with you."

Were Cath and I wrong for each from the start? Even back during the days when we thought things were right? As proven by the fact that while at home living with me she couldn't even feel comfortable enough to bond with our dog?

I was suddenly overcome by a powerful sense of dread, and it had nothing to do with our missing sun.

With Scout right behind me, wagging his tail excitedly, I returned to the living room and noticed the TV remote on the floor. Anthony was always leaving it there. He liked to sprawl out on the floor in front of the TV and hold onto the remote. I grabbed it, saying, "Before we go, let's see what's going on out there."

We were greeted by the image of a darkened city, New York as it turned out. It looked as if it were in the middle of the night. Buildings were lit, as were the headlights of the bumper to bumper cars which slowly crawled along the busy street.

Then came the voice-over of the veteran newscaster.

"What you're seeing now is our camera outside the studio. Darkness has fallen all over the land on this afternoon of July 13th. Reports coming in tell us that this is happening all over the world, that the entire world is shrouded in darkness. Difficult to believe but apparently true. The temperature has also begun to drop dramatically, approaching freezing in some parts of the country. Still no word yet from the White House—"

There was more, but all of it speculation.

"Enough of this," I muttered in disappointment. I wanted answers. "Let's bring Lara home."

Scout barked.

"Yeah, you can come, too," I told him.

Lara lived about 5 miles from our house, on the other side of Barlow Village, the quaint little New Hampshire town in which we lived.

It was normally a ten-minute drive. However, the weather had become nasty, and it took us much longer.

Storm strength winds blew the trees nearly horizontal. Hail pelted the windshield in a tremendous deluge, reducing visibility to nil, even with the wipers at full blast.

When we pulled into her driveway, her house was dark.

I looked over my shoulder at the boys. "I'm going in with Lara. You guys stay here."

"Can we come in, too?" they both asked.

"I'd rather you didn't."

"Please???"

"We don't want to be alone!" Sean added.

I couldn't blame them. In events such as this one, people just aren't meant to be alone.

"All right, then," I said, as Scout barked. "Sorry, but I draw the line with you. Stay! We'll be right back."

We ran from the minivan to Lara's house as hail the size of rabbit pellets pelted our heads. Lara opened the screen door, and we all piled into the house, our hair and clothes covered with an icy coat of hail that clung to us the way snow clings to a tree during a spring snowstorm. Sean and Anthony looked at their bodies.

"We look like robots," Anthony giggled.

Lara called for her mom. There wasn't an answer.

She flicked on the lights, and we made a quick check of the house. No one was home.

"This is unexpected," I said.

"She wasn't planning on being gone long, or she would have left a note," Lara said.

Why didn't I think of that? A note back at our house letting Lara's mom know where we were in case she was there right now looking for Lara.

"Maybe she took your brothers somewhere?" I suggested.

"Maybe."

"And your dad's at work?" I asked.

She nodded.

A gust of wind rattled the windows.

Lara jumped. She looked terribly afraid.

This wasn't a time to be alone.

"We'll stay with you for a while, if you'd like," I said.

"Are you sure?" she asked.

"Sure. You guys want stay here with Lara until her mom comes back?"

They cheered.

"Well, that settles that," I said.

So we waited, but the longer we waited without anyone returning home, the more I thought of Cath, and I kept kicking myself for not having left a note. Cath could have been at our house right then, and she wouldn't have had any idea where we were. Of course, I didn't really believe Cath was home. Common sense told me she was busy at work in the ER. Yet, emotions disintegrate common sense like acid.

"Lara, we need to get back to our house just in case Cath comes back home," I said. "Why don't you come with us?"

She shook her head. "No. I should be here."

"Are you sure?"

She nodded, but she looked far from convincing.

"You could leave your parents a note. They'd know you're safe," I pressed the issue. It was clear the girl was terribly frightened.

Sean and Anthony chimed in. "Please? Won't you stay with us?"

"You don't mind?" Lara asked.

"Mind? On a day like today, the more company the better," I smiled.

Lara found a pad and pencil by the telephone and scribbled a note to her parents. She left it on the kitchen table.

Opening the screen door to leave the house, we stopped short. The hail had changed to snow.

The ride back to our house from Lara's was even slower than before, not only because of the blizzard like conditions, but because there was now bumper to bumper traffic on the road, which was unheard of around here. Barlow Village was an extremely small town. Traffic here didn't exist. Yet, today the road was full, a genuine caravan of cars, minivans, pick-up trucks, SUVs, and tractor trailers. It looked like a mass exodus from one of those 1950s giant monster movies.

"Where is everyone going?" Sean asked.

"Either home, or they're leaving," I answered.

"Why would they be leaving?" Sean asked again.

I'd been asking myself the same question, and I didn't like the answer.

House after house, we saw nothing but darkness. People were leaving.

We pulled into our driveway. I had held the faintest hope that I'd see Cath's Volvo in the driveway. I didn't, and the arteries around my heart tightened.

We quickly ran through the pouring snow to the dry confines of the screened-in porch.

Entering the house, the kids stumbled on ahead of Lara and me, with Scout dutifully bringing up the rear, and Anthony bellowed his usual, "Home, sweet home!"

"He's not really aware of what's going on. Good," I thought, but I knew better than to think the same of Sean. He was eight, and he was very aware of what was going on. I could see it in his eyes, the raw fear.

Yet, like children the world over, Sean possessed the amazing ability to roll with the punches and cope with just about anything, anything that is, but a parental breakup. He had not handled that well at all, and to my surprise, his whole attitude towards me had changed. He had grown much colder, as if he blamed me for driving Cath away, which, to an extent, was true. I was the reason Cath left.

I closed the door behind us and flicked on the light switch. The light didn't go on.

"Uh oh," I said.

"What?" Sean asked nervously.

"I think the power's out." I tried a lamp. Same result.

The boys were suddenly running around trying all the lights they could touch.

"Yep! The power's out!" they both announced.

"Daddy, I'm cold!" Anthony whined.

"That's because you left all the windows open!" Sean said to me, and I knew from the tone of his voice that he wanted to add the word "idiot." Attitude again.

This whole Sean thing had caught me off guard, especially since he and I had always been extremely close. Like any parent, I would honestly say that I loved both my children the same, yet

I can't deny the special bond that has always existed between myself and my first born son. Some unspoken connection, some spark, that brings us together in a way that I can't explain nor completely understand other than to know it's there.

I had had this experience once before, with my paternal grandfather. We too shared an unspoken connection that seemed to make us soul mates for life, and if dear old grampa can be believed, after death as well. During the last years of his life when he was really ill, he had been fond of saying to me, "We'll be together again. Just like old times. You and I, running around a baseball field."

Soul mates. Not with my parents. Not even with Cath. I'd only felt this bond with grampa. Until Sean came along. And then it was there again.

I knew it to be real because it wasn't something I sought. It just was.

So when he turned on me, not only didn't I expect it, but it hurt all the worse.

"Well, it is July!" I barked in response. "And it was 80 degrees this morning! Give me a break!"

Sean swallowed. Hurt.

I began closing the windows, and as Lara and the boys helped, we soon had the house sealed shut. Yet it was still damned cold inside, and it didn't help that we were wearing shorts and t-shirts.

I checked the thermostat. The inside temperature had already dropped to its lowest point, 40 degrees. It felt even colder, which it probably was. The thermostat didn't record temperatures lower than forty, and with the power out, the furnace wouldn't be turning on any time soon.

Our winter clothes were stacked away in boxes in the basement, with the exception of our winter coats, which hung in the front closet.

"Guys, you'd better put these on," I said, entering the living room with a stack of coats over my arm.

"Winter coats in the summer?" Sean asked.

"That's silly!" Anthony laughed.

"I wish it were," I thought, as I handed Lara one of Cath's coats.

We sat in the dim living room, lit by the flickering light of the one candle we kept on hand in case of blackouts, all bundled up in our coats, talking occasionally but mostly sitting in silence. The snow continued to fall outside, and the howling winds shook the windows with a ferocity usually seen only in the worst winter storms.

I craved news. I wanted to know what had happened, and what was being done about it, but without power, our television was useless.

"How about the radio?" Sean asked.

"No batteries," I said.

"The van's got a radio," Sean said. "And heat!"

He was right on both counts, the smart aleck. Actually, I appreciated his smarts.

"You guys want to go into the van for a bit? Warm up. Hear some news?" I said.

The answer was a big "yes." Even Scout barked and wagged his tail.

Once again, we paraded out the front door onto the porch and into the snow-covered yard. Several inches of the white stuff had fallen onto the ground, and our sneakers, out of their league, provided our feet with little protection from the wintry elements. In short, as we made our way to the driveway, our feet were wet and cold.

I was just about to open the side door to the van to let the kids inside when a deafening boom exploded in the sky above our heads. It was the kind of sound that brings grown men to their knees. Anthony shrieked and fell flat on his back into the snow as if someone had knocked him off his feet, a comical sight if not for the circumstances. I looked up into the sky, not sure what I expected to see. Fire, perhaps? Scout yelped and then howled. I didn't see anything in the sky. I turned towards Anthony, but Lara was already helping him up.

Then Sean cried out, "Look!"

I followed my son's pointing finger to see way off in the distance what looked to be monstrous flashes of light, red flashes, igniting the entire sky, looking like something out of *War of the Worlds*.

"In the van!" I shouted, and I rushed everyone inside. I followed right behind and slid the side door shut. As Lara buckled up the boys, and Scout hopped into the rear seat, I inserted myself behind the wheel, started her up, blasted the heat, and turned on the radio.

Anthony was crying. I looked back to see Lara removing him from his car seat and carrying him with her to the farthest seat in the back. As she sat Anthony on her lap, she rocked him gently in order to soothe him.

Seeing that the front passenger seat was unoccupied, Scout jumped down from his position next to Lara and Anthony, and squeezing his way by Lara's legs, scurried to the front seat where he joined me by my side, his front paws up on the dash, and his tail wagging behind.

"I don't want to die!" Sean cried, his voice full of panic.

"You're not going to die!" I said, and I quickly turned up the volume on the radio.

"—that was the President just moments ago from the White House saying that as of right now, no evidence exists that this is a terrorist act. He also made it clear that they just don't know. The belief out there right now, at least from the few scientists we've heard from, is that the sun is gone. I'll say that again because the very notion is—well, how else can I say it? It's far-fetched and unbelievable, but they're saying it's true. The sun is gone."

My breathing grew erratic. I could feel the pressure mounting around my chest.

"What do they mean the sun is gone?" Sean cried. "That's impossible! The sun can't be gone! We can't live without the sun!"

"All right, Sean, take it easy! They don't know! Okay?" I barked. "They don't really know. They're just guessing!"

I changed the station. I wanted local news. I wanted to know what the hell was going on in the sky all around us. I stopped when I heard the panicked voice of a newscaster.

"Authorities are urging people to stay in their homes and take shelter in their basements. Heavy meteor showers are now being reported over the skies all across the United States.

Extensive damage has been reported, especially in the Seattle, Washington area, and more recently, in northern New England. The states of Maine, New Hampshire, and Vermont have all reported heavy meteorite activity."

Another bright flash lit up the sky.

"Are those the meteorites?" Sean asked.

"—authorities are urging people not to panic, to seek shelter in their basements or in the many public shelters being set up in cities and towns across the country. We are told that huge multitudes of people are taking to the nation's highways, and that this is causing a very dangerous situation. So please, if you can, stay home—"

Stay home?

That was the last thing I wanted to do.

Those red flashes in the sky were coming from the east. From Concord. Where Cath was working.

If only she'd come around the corner in her Volvo and pull into the driveway, I found myself thinking. That would solve everything. That would make everything right. We could retreat to the cellar as a family and hide out together. We'd be able to focus our energies on the disaster at hand.

Focus. That was something I was having trouble with. In the van with my children and Lara, I was only partially there. The other part was with Cath.

"Come home, Cath," I whispered, as if willing her to return.

"She's not coming home!" my conscience groaned. "Get over it! Get over her!"

"How can I get over her? She's still my wife! We're not divorced yet! I still love her. Despite everything, I still love her!"

I looked at the gas gauge. Three quarters full. Plenty of gas for a trip to Concord.

"Guys? I'm not sure what to do, but I think I want to go to the hospital and find mommy," I said, my voice tentative, my emotions confused. "And I think I should go alone."

"No! No, dad! Please!" Sean yelled in a voice full of horror, as if the notion of separating from another parent would strike him down dead on the spot.

"Driving right now is dangerous!" I argued.

"Then don't go! Let's go down to the cellar! That's what the man on the radio said to do!" Sean said.

"But what about mom?" I asked, and it was a rhetorical question, because I was thinking these things out as I was speaking.

"I want to get mommy! Let's go get mommy!" Anthony cried from the back seat.

"It's too dangerous! We can't go!" Sean shouted at his brother.

Life is full of bad decisions, and I guess this is part of what makes us human. So often we can see the writing on the wall in huge letters in red ink, "DON'T DO THAT!" yet we do it anyway.

I knew I'd be putting my children and Lara in jeopardy, but the fact of the matter was, I had to find Cath, and I wasn't about to separate myself from my children. So, common sense be damned!

I turned halfway to look at Sean, Lara, and Anthony.

"I want to find mom," I said. "We'll go together. Lara, I'll take you home first."

She squeezed Anthony tightly and shook her head.

"No," she said. "I'll go with you."

"Are you sure?"

She nodded.

People aren't meant to be alone.

"All right, let's do it then," I said.

I backed the van onto the road which was already thick with snow- the snow plows hadn't mobilized yet, and on a day like today, who's to say they even would? Traffic had dissipated somewhat. There was now only an occasional car on the road, and most of them were slipping, sliding, or worse yet, stuck. I hadn't even driven a quarter mile and I was already second-guessing myself.

"How can you do this to your children? Put them in danger like this? You coward! Just because you can't bear to be without your wife, the same woman who walked out on you! You pathetic excuse for a man!" My conscience was without mercy.

We merged onto Interstate 89 for the drive to Concord. This

was a stretch of highway I usually raced along at 75 miles per hour, but at this moment I was lucky to be doing twenty. The windshield wipers were at full blast, but I still couldn't see a thing. That's how fast the snow was falling. There was a car in front of us, so I focused on its red rear lights and nothing else.

Flashes were lighting up the sky all over the place, and even inside the sealed van, we could hear the thunderous booms.

About three miles outside Concord, the red rear lights of the car in front of us brightened. Brake lights. The car was stopping. Up ahead through the whiteout conditions I could barely make out the wild flashing of blue police lights.

"Why are we stopping?" Anthony asked from way in the back.

"The police are in the road. Might be an accident," I answered. I noticed movement in the road ahead. Cars seemed to be turning around. "Uh oh."

"What?" Sean asked.

"I think they're making us turn around."

I watched as the car in front of us, a green station wagon it looked like, began the process of a three point turn. Suddenly, as if out of thin air, a tall state trooper dressed in a thick parka emerged from the white background and approached my window, which I quickly rolled down. Scout offered a low growl as the officer stepped towards the van.

"Quiet, Scout," I muttered.

"You need to turn around, sir," the officer said.

"We're on our way to Concord," I tried to say, but the officer cut me short.

"The city's closed. You've got to turn around."

"But my wife—" I pointed over my shoulder. "Their mom—"

"The city is closed. Now turn around. Immediately, sir. Let's go!" he shouted.

"No, you don't understand. My wife is in the city. I need—"

He leaned his head deep into my window, into my personal space. "Listen to me. What you need is to get your kids out of here! Do you hear what I'm saying? It's a state of emergency! The city is gone, and in a few minutes, this whole area is going to be engulfed in flame. Turn around, and get the hell out of here! Now move!"

He slapped at my door as he moved on to the next car behind us. I was shaking.

"What does he mean the city is gone?" Sean asked. "Is mommy all right? Are we going to see mommy?"

I didn't answer. I was too busy trembling. At that moment I stopped thinking and switched to "automatic pilot" mode. I began turning the van around, which was no easy task in the storm, especially the drive over the median to get to the northbound lane. Once I had turned around, I drove out of there as quickly as I could, which, with all the snow both on the ground and still falling, wasn't speedy at all.

I had driven maybe two miles when Sean screamed out, "Daddy, watch out!"

I looked up. A flaming ball of fire, huge, the size of a house, passed right over us from right to left and landed in the woods across the highway, setting off what sounded like a sonic boom and igniting the whole area in a fiery inferno. Anthony shrieked liked he was being dismembered, and Scout began an incessant howl.

As more balls of fire fell, landing all around us, I tried desperately to get us out of there, but the thick snow clung to the van's tires, and moving fast just wasn't an option.

"Come on, come on!" I muttered. "Just get us back home."

While in the air, the meteorites rumbled, like thunder. Right off the bat, the newest rumble differed. Not only was it much louder, but it possessed the added element of a whistle. It didn't take me long to place the sound, and by then, I was ready to shriek myself. I looked up as far into the front windshield as I could.

"Oh no," I moaned. "I can't see it. I don't know where it is!"

"Can't see what?" Sean screeched.

The rumbling was now a full-blown roar, so menacingly loud the entire van shook and rattled. Scout jumped down and hid underneath the dashboard, his tail between his legs. Anthony was crying outright, and checking the rear-view mirror, I saw Lara's face full of tears as well.

"What is it???" Sean hollered.

I clenched my fists tightly to the steering wheel, gritted my teeth and ducked my head low, applying my foot to the brake. I was too shaken up to drive, and then it passed directly overhead.

A passenger jet, humongous, probably a 767, a mother of a plane, flying so low I knew it was going to crash.

"Sweet mother of Jesus!" I cried.

I slammed my foot on the brake and brought us to a complete stop. The enormous aircraft was about to belly flop directly in front of us.

"It's going to crash!" I screamed. "Close your eyes!"

Lara covered Anthony's and shut her own, while Sean turned his head but couldn't avert his eyes. Like son, like father. I felt like the ultimate reality TV fiend, horrified yet glued to the screen. Why do horror and the disasters which befall humanity fascinate us so much?

The plane went down, several hundred yards ahead of us, into the forest beyond the curving highway. I grimaced and clenched my teeth, as I watched the airliner plunge to the earth.

There was a flash, and then the whole thing went up. Three explosions in quick succession, loud and horrifying, and we all screamed. These three explosions converged into one gigantic fireball that climbed into the sky like a towering skyscraper.

Another meteorite fell, real close, to our left, shaking the hell out of the earth.

I thought we were going to die, but I told myself, "We're less than a mile from the Barlow Village exit. We're almost home!"

Trembling, I pressed my foot to the gas pedal and inched our van forward, through the snow, past the fires, by the meteorite hits, until we reached the exit.

I guided the van onto the off ramp and headed into town.

We got as far as the Town Hall when the road became too thick with snow to be passable. We had to stop.

I pulled up behind a line of cars which had been left in front of the Hall. I hoped that perhaps the town had set up a shelter inside.

I ushered everyone out of the van and led them towards

the Hall. I didn't have a leash for Scout, but he made like my shadow and followed me closely all the way into the building, and no one said anything about his presence.

Once inside, we were immediately directed to the staircase which led down to the underground bunker, originally designed as a bomb shelter during the cold war.

The room was crowded with residents of Barlow Village, and I tell you honestly, never have I been so happy to see so many familiar faces. Among them, I saw Pam Dooley, huddled with her two children Mark and Melissa, playmates of Sean and Anthony, and we headed in their direction. Her husband Jim wasn't with them.

"He's in Europe," Pam said. "We tried to call him and actually got through, but the phones went out."

"I'm sorry," I said. Pam looked so sad. I asked if she had seen Cath, but she hadn't, and that was the extent of our conversation, as we were too exhausted and scared to say much of anything else.

The room was full of people, yet it was quiet, with just hushed murmurings here and there. We sounded like a church gathering before the service, until Morgan Belieau, the town manager, called for everyone's attention. They had set up a podium, and although there was no microphone, Morgan, a gifted public speaker, projected his voice sufficiently so that even those of us in the back could still hear what he had to say.

"The good news is the meteor showers seem to be over. The bad news is the weather. The conditions outside remain life threatening. The temperature has dropped well below zero, and the snow drifts are covering the cars. We strongly advise everyone who's here to remain here, for your own safety. We have plenty of food stored down here, and bottled water."

"How long?" someone asked. "How long can we stay down here? How much supplies do we have?"

"What about fresh air?" someone else asked.

Morgan nodded affirmatively and moved his arms in a downward motion, his body language definitely implying "it's OK. Keep calm."

"We have enough food to accommodate a crowd this size

for a month, and believe me, if we're here that long, we will have come up with an alternative plan by then, I guarantee you. As far as fresh air is concerned, there is a vent system in place, and it is operating. It's powered by the same generator which is giving us our light and our heat.

"If any one of you at any time wants to leave," Morgan continued, "that's your call, and no one here will stop you, but we strongly recommend you stay."

I immediately thought of Cath, separated from those who loved her most. I had failed to find her. I looked into Sean's nervous eyes, and it was almost as if he were reading my mind. For a moment, I wanted to go out there and try again, but looking into my son's eyes, I knew I couldn't. I couldn't take them into harm's way again, nor could I leave them to search for Cath alone.

Some time later, Cliff Rogers, the head postal clerk in town and other than Morgan Belieau the most visible public leader and closest thing to a mayor Barlow Village had, came up behind me and placed his hand on my shoulder. He whispered, "We've made an executive decision. The pets can't stay."

I could feel my face contorting into a scowl that would have made Clint Eastwood proud.

"Who made an executive decision?" I asked.

"Morgan, myself, and the other civic leaders who are here. We all love pets, but there's a limited amount of food and water. Only enough for the people."

I'd never liked Cliff Rogers much. There was something cold about him. With his neatly trimmed yet thick mustache and goatee, and his serious demeanor, he came across more like a high school principal than a postal clerk. Even the way he sold you stamps made you feel you were under his watchful eye, or at least he made me feel that way. Yet he was one of the most popular men in town. "He does so much for the village" was a popular refrain you heard when someone was talking about Cliff Rogers, and it was true. There wasn't a project in town that Cliff didn't become involved with, from fighting to keep truck traffic through the village to a minimum to rolling up his sleeves to build the new children's playground. The man was ubiquitous.

He was still a cold fish with me though. I always got the

feeling he looked down upon me because I didn't have a "real" job, but then again, I guess I'm hypersensitive about that. Anyway, he was rubbing me the wrong way once again.

"It's the kids' dog," I lied.

Cliff glanced down at Scout and then over at Anthony, who was sitting on Lara's lap, and then at Sean who was standing with Mark and Melissa, before looking back at me.

"I'm sorry. They'll understand."

"That's easy for you to say, you cold-hearted bastard! You don't have to tell them!" I thought.

"Would you like me to do it?" he asked.

"Do what?"

"You need to put him down. It's the humane thing to do."

I looked at him with what I'm sure was a horrified expression on my face. "You mean kill him?" I asked, careful to keep my voice down.

"He'll freeze to death out there. That's a lousy way to go. A painful way to go."

Damn Rogers for being right!

But Scout was a member of our family. We loved him. I loved him. I couldn't.

I have a knack for making the wrong decisions, and it's because I'm a very emotional person, and my emotions often dominate my thinking processes as well as my actions. I often know something "should" be done, but I decide against it because my heart says otherwise. It's cliché, but I've been told I have a very feminine way of thinking. I guess it's that stay at home dad thing again.

There was no way that I or anyone else was going to shoot Scout. The dog deserved the chance to fight for his survival. This was my heart talking. My head was telling me the dog would die a gruesome, painful death out there in the cold, and he would definitely suffer.

What kind of a man did that make me, that I would let my dog suffer? A coward. My conscience talking again, and it added, "Another reason your wife left you. You're a slave to your emotions. You wouldn't know a good decision if it kicked you in the ass!"

It's a problem I never used to have. Staying home with my kids simply made me a more emotional person than I used to be, and it's because children are like crossword puzzles, except instead of exercising the mind, they exercise the emotions. On the one hand, they elicit pure joy by doing the sweet funny things kids do, and on the other, as extremely irrational beings, they plain and simply put their parents through emotional hell. Hang around kids, you sweat emotion.

"No," I said, staring emptily into space before turning to Rogers. "I'll do it."

He nodded contemplatively. "Sooner than later. We want to finish the purge as soon as possible."

Before I could say "screw you!" he pumped my hand with a firm handshake and said, "See me if you need anything," and he was on his way, making his rounds through the crowd.

I was trembling. I didn't want to explain Scout's fate to Sean or Anthony, nor did I want to do what I was going to have to do. I should have let Rogers do it.

Wrong decision #9,342.

I called Sean over. Anthony's eyes naturally followed his brother towards me.

"Guys," I said weakly. "Scout can't stay here with us. This place is just for people not for pets. I've got to take him outside."

"He'll die outside," Sean said.

I was too exhausted to be creative. "We don't have a choice."

"I don't want Scout to die!" Anthony cried.

"I don't want him to die either!" I said, with an unfortunate edge in my voice. "I've got to take him now."

"I want to go with you," Sean said.

"Me, too!" Anthony cried.

And now for wrong decision #9,343.

"Okay."

Scout was sitting by my feet, looking directly up at me. As he so often did, he looked at me with an expression that made me think he had understood every word of which had just been spoken. His eyes were so sad.

"Come on, Scout," I said, feeling terrible, and the four of us walked to the staircase which ascended to ground level.

Once inside the spacious main room of the town hall, we saw Morgan Belieau standing by the front door next to a couple of other men, all of whom were wrapped in thick winter coats and hats. The wind was howling, and the hall full of drafts.

"My boys just want to say good-bye to the family dog," I said to Morgan once we had reached him.

He nodded. "Okay. Once we open the door, don't be out there for more than a minute." He looked at me expectantly, and I knew what he was looking for.

"We don't believe in guns in our family," I said.

He looked at me the way I would expect a doctor to look at a Christian Scientist. Unlike Cliff Rogers, Morgan Belieau, with his warm smile, soft eyes and smooth silver hair, was very much the grandfatherly type. He had a way of making people feel good about themselves all the time, and when he disagreed with you, he let you know without cutting you down. "It's your dog, and you know what's best for him. Let me know when you want us to open the door."

He motioned for the two other men to join him across the hall.

"Why did you say we don't believe in guns in our family?" Sean asked.

"Because—they don't want Scout to suffer."

Sean thought about this for a minute but still didn't get it.

"They want me to shoot Scout so he won't suffer out there in the cold."

Both Sean's and Anthony's eyes went full moon wide, and Anthony dropped to his knees and wrapped his arms around Scout's neck. "You're not going to shoot Scout!"

"No, I'm not going to shoot him."

"Then he's going to suffer," I heard Sean say, and his voice was as cold as the wind howling outside. We made eye contact, and once again, I could see his disappointment and anger focused upon me.

"I'm not a coward, Sean. I'm an optimist, and I will be an optimist until I die. I believe Scout deserves the chance to survive out there, and I'm giving him that chance."

Sean opened his mouth to comment but evidently changed

his mind, because he didn't say anything.

I said, "All right, let's say good-bye to Scout."

"Bye, Scout," Anthony said, showering his neck with kisses. Sean crouched to one knee and did the same.

"Okay, dad's turn," I said.

I crouched down and hugged the poor dog. His smooth fur, which even when clean used to smell bad and drive my sensitive nose crazy, smelled so familiar now, like home. I hugged him close and could feel his heart beating.

"I love you, Scout," I whispered. "God how I wish it were true you could understand me. This isn't my choice. I'd keep you with us forever. I don't want to send you out there. You're a good dog."

I stood and told Morgan Belieau we were ready to open the door. He came over, motioned for the boys to step back a bit, and making sure I was ready, opened the door.

A blast of cold air struck our faces, and it took my breath away.

"Bring him out. Quickly!" Belieau urged.

I nudged Scout towards the door, but he wanted no part of the outside, and plunked his butt down on the floor. He wouldn't move. I reached underneath his belly and pushed upwards, and Scout responded, standing on all fours.

"Come on Scout!" I beckoned, but he still wasn't moving.

I wrapped my arms around his body and carried him out the door. The kids started to follow me, and I heard Morgan call them back. I plopped Scout onto the snowy ground, and when he landed, he immediately dropped his tail between his legs. For a moment, he faced the snowy unknown, before turning his head to look back at me. With his ears low and his face wrinkled into a frown, his body language screamed, "Why are you doing this to me?"

I hated myself at that moment. I stood with him for a short time, out there in the blizzard. Snow was swirling everywhere, and it was blindingly white. I couldn't see a thing beyond three feet of me.

"I love you, Scout. You're a good dog!" I shouted. "Now go home! Go home, Scout! Go home!"

I bent over and kissed him on the top of his head. I turned around and nearly bumped into Morgan, as he was holding the door open for me. I stepped back into the hall and looked over my shoulder one last time. Scout was still standing there, looking at me with that confused, depressed look in his eye, and then Morgan Belieau slammed the door shut.

There were about three-hundred of us cramped inside the underground bunker, about half the population of Barlow Village. It was windowless, of course, yet the lighting was adequate, even bright, and there was a ventilation system. Air continued to flow throughout the room, and although it wasn't comparable to having the windows open on a balmy summer afternoon, it sufficed.

Belieau assured us again that the generator would not fail, but added that even if it did, we wouldn't freeze to death, since the temperature underground remained constant, around 55 degrees Fahrenheit, I think he said.

There were bathrooms, so basic washing and bathroom needs would be taken care of.

We were all exhausted, yet most of us were talking nonstop, a result of nervous energy, I suppose. Talking and speculating.

About what had happened.

Had the sun actually been struck by terrorists? Had it simply died out long before scientists assumed it would? Was God fed up with the human race?

"You can rule out terrorists," said Jim McIntyre, an elderly man we knew through church, a really nice guy. He always patted the boys on their heads and made a point to ask Sean how the Red Sox were doing. Jim was sitting in our group, which consisted of me, Lara, the boys, Pam Dooley and her kids, Mrs. Carrigan, our neighbor who lived three houses down the street, and a husband and wife who looked to be in their early thirty's who I didn't know.

"I was talking to my son on the telephone shortly after this happened. He's an astronomer," Jim said. "I told him I thought it was terrorists, but he said even the most powerful man made weapon, the hydrogen bomb, wouldn't affect the sun."

"Why not?" the husband asked, looking like he had just sucked on a lemon.

"I'm not sure exactly," Jim answered. "Something about a bomb being the same kind of mechanism by which the sun radiates."

"It'd be like throwing fire on fire," I said.

"Yeah, I guess that's about right," Jim nodded.

"What about an asteroid collision?" the wife asked.

Jim shook his head. "I thought of that too, but Jimmy said no. Said it would have to be huge. Even something the size of Jupiter, he said, wouldn't knock her out. Anything large enough to knock out the sun would most likely destroy the entire solar system at the same time, and since we're still here, that's not the case."

"Maybe it just burnt itself out, then," Sean said.

"Jimmy didn't think so," Jim answered.

"Maybe Jimmy doesn't know what the hell he's talking about!" the husband said. "I still think it's freakin terrorists! Those Muslims are clever bastards!"

I threw a contemptuous glare the husband's way. He looked like the kind of guy who came home from work, cracked open a can of beer, farted, and waited for his wife to cook him dinner without lifting a finger to help her.

She grabbed his arm and nestled close to him. Poor thing, I thought, to be stuck with a guy like that.

Then the irony of my thought smacked me in the face. He's the guy with a wife on his arm!

"What are you looking at?" the husband asked when he noticed I was staring at him.

My favorite response to this question has always been my best friend's from the 6th grade, Stevie Mullen. He'd say, doing his best George Jefferson impersonation, "I haven't figured out yet!"

I had nothing so clever or dramatic up my sleeve.

"What does it look like? I'm looking at you," I said.

"Well, knock it the hell off, all right?"

"Why? What are you going to do? Ask me to step outside?"

"Don't be a wise ass!" he said continuing to display all his charm.

"Dad," Sean said. I looked at my son, and he whispered, "Stop it, okay."

As much as I wanted to tell this guy off, I knew Sean was right. It wouldn't solve anything, and it would only make matters worse, so I smiled at Sean and stopped talking to Mr. Potato Head.

"I agree with you. Terrorists are clever," Jim said. "But Jimmy made it quite clear. Nothing here on earth—"

"Screw *Jimmy*, already! What the hell does he know!" Mr. Potato Head said.

"He's got a Ph.D.," Jim muttered.

"All book smarts is all that is! No common sense!"

I rolled my eyes and looked over at Jim. We exchanged smiles of disbelief.

"Did he say anything about what he thought might have happened?" I asked Jim.

"He did," Jim answered, and Mr. Potato Head groaned, as if to say, "Here it comes!" "He said something about a—what did he call it now? A magnetic a-nom-a-ly, I think. This a-nom-a-ly, theoretically, could disturb the way the sun shines. He gave me more details, but it was all over my head. He also mentioned something about interstellar dust, but he said that was unlikely too because it would have to be large, and the scientists of the world would have seen it coming a long time ago."

"Well maybe they weren't looking too carefully!" Potato Head complained.

"Those theories are all fine, Jim," Mrs. Carrigan said, "but the fact remains, the sun isn't shining anymore. *Something* happened up there, and if your son Jimmy, a scientist, doesn't know what—well, I just don't like the sound of it."

"Does it really matter what happened?" Pam Dooley asked. "It's over and done with! We have to think about our survival now!" And she hugged her two children.

"Survival?" Potato Head said. "Lady, with the sun gone, we ain't surviving! I don't need no Ph.D. to tell me that!"

Thanks to his lame-brained comment, the children lost all color in their faces. I was ready to say "shut up!" but Jim said calmly, "I don't think the sun is gone." There was a confidence in his voice I found soothing. "I'm reasonably certain if it had been destroyed, we wouldn't be here right now."

"Well, where the hell is it? Playing hide and seek?" the husband asked.

"I don't know," Jim answered. "For some reason, it has stopped shining, but it's still up there, and I believe it will shine again."

No one, not even Potato Head, wanted to add anything more after such an optimistic statement. The conversation ended right there, which is exactly where we wanted it to end, and we sat in a contemplative perhaps even prayerful silence for a long time.

A short time later, someone mentioned that Morgan Belieau and Cliff Rogers had access to a radio. The next time Belieau took to the podium, Jim McIntyre wanted to know what was going on out there.

"What are they saying on the radio?" Jim asked.

"Nothing much," Belieau answered. "Still don't know what happened."

"Is the president all right?" asked Mrs. Carrigan.

"Yes, the president is all right," Belieau said, a statement which caused the folks in the room to erupt in loud burst of hoots and applause. The reaction brought a smile to Belieau's face. "He's in an undisclosed location, but he keeps delivering radio messages every couple of hours or so."

"What's he saying?" Jim asked

"For us not to give up. For us not to lose hope. For us to remember that we're Americans," Belieau said. "He also said something else, something I thought was very poignant. He said we should remember that we're human beings, and that the human race which populates this world is full of brilliant minds and miracle workers, and that with God's help, we will find an answer, and we will survive."

The room erupted in a thunderous cheer.

The first and second days passed without a hitch, but by day three people were growing stir crazy. Not being able to see the sun, not being able to breathe fresh air, not being able to change one's underwear, by the third day these things were starting to make us testy and uncomfortable.

It was on this day that Morgan Belieau decided to let people back up to the main level once again, to shake things up a bit.

When it was our turn, we bundled ourselves up in our winter coats and trekked over to the staircase. Lara hung close to the boys, and Jim McIntyre came along in our group as well.

McIntyre patted Sean on the head. "Figures something like this would happen this summer, with the Red Sox in first place over the Yankees!"

Before allowing us entry into the main lobby of the town hall, Morgan Belieau warned us to keep away from the windows and the door, and for us not to remove our coats or hats.

"The cold is like nothing you've ever experienced," he said.

When he opened the door to let us inside the hall, the cold that blasted through the doorway was like some kind of pouncing animal, pressing hard against our bodies and nearly ripping the door from its hinges. We were actually forced back several steps, and Anthony lost his balance and fell on his butt.

"Quickly!" Belieau beckoned. "We need to close this door to keep the cold from getting down to the bunker!"

Lara picked Anthony up, and we all trudged into the main room.

"Good God!" McIntyre said, as Belieau closed the door behind us.

It was as if we had walked into a hall full of ghosts. White whispery things flew all around us like spectral apparitions, eerily lit by the numerous battery operated lamps placed at even intervals around the room, but these were no ghosts. Snow and ice, nothing more, blown around the hall in an indoor squall.

The ground and walls were white with icy snow. The windows had all been boarded up. The staircase which led to the second level had also been blocked by nailed boards.

"It's so goddamned cold even with everything boarded up we can't keep the moisture out," Belieau said.

"How cold is it?" I asked.

"It was fifty below yesterday before the thermometer broke," Cliff Rogers said, approaching us from the boarded up front door.

"Any theories yet? What are they saying on the radio?" McIntyre asked.

Neither man answered.

"What is it?" I asked.

Belieau ushered us away from the kids.

"We haven't picked up any broadcasts in the past twelve hours," he said.

Both men looked grim.

"You don't think we're going to make it, do you?" McIntyre asked.

"Do you?" Rogers asked with that cold edge in his voice.

"We have food and water for a month," McIntyre said.

"Three-hundred people in one room will never survive a month," Rogers said.

"You're awfully pessimistic," McIntyre said.

"Care to share any reason why I shouldn't be?"

"I believe in God," McIntyre said.

"Don't get me started on God!" Rogers said.

"I didn't know you weren't a religious man, Cliff," McIntyre said.

"I used to be."

"What happened?"

"God never shows up. Ever notice he's always conspicuously absent every time there's a tragedy?" Rogers asked. "Hell, he's always absent! Good times, bad, it doesn't matter. Anyone ever see God? No, and you know why? He's not there!"

"Once you have faith, you understand," McIntyre said calmly.

"Faith? That's code for God doesn't exist so you'd better believe in the idea of him!"

"Gentlemen, this conversation isn't going to help matters," Belieau said in his grandfatherly tone. "We will all be better served by a cautious sense of optimism."

"Amen," McIntyre nodded.

The conversation changed course, with Belieau going on at length about our ample supplies and heat. In the bunker, we were safe from the elements, he said, but that's not what concerned him. He and Rogers were worried about our psychological health, and they conceded that we would need to venture outside at some point, probably sooner than later.

I found myself too preoccupied with my own anxieties to be

an active participant in the conversation. As such, I missed most of what they were saying.

Instead, I kept looking at my boys, playing with Lara, and I kept thinking, "I don't want them to die as children. I want them to live, be happy, and enjoy their childhood so they can grow into well-balanced men who will do right by the world."

I heard the words "suicide pills" and focused in on Belieau saying they had them, but they weren't about to use them. Rogers was going on about "dying with dignity."

I wasn't handing my kids suicide pills. I thought of Scout and saw the dreadful image of the dog lying in the snow, the cold so harsh it sliced open slits in the dog's body drawing bright red blood.

"How many times? Before you stop making the same mistakes?" my conscience asked.

I thought of Catherine. How she had left after all those years of marriage, an action I'd never pegged her for taking. My life was one big mistake.

I felt a soft tug on my hand and turned to see Sean by my side. He pulled me away from the trio of men.

"Dad, what's a suicide pill?" Sean whispered.

The question hit me like a burst of ammonia.

For as long as I could remember, I had never lied to Sean or Anthony. I had always felt strongly about treating my sons as mature beings and with respect. Now, as I thought about it, it just seemed like one more mistake.

"Do you know what suicide is?" I asked him.

He nodded. "When you kill yourself."

"That's what a suicide pill does."

Sean pointed to the men behind me. "Why do they want that?"

I grimaced, and I could feel my face hardening, as if I were aging ten years right before Sean's eyes. I crouched down and spoke to him at eye level. "The thinking is, being trapped down here with no hope of escape, might drive people crazy, or if we run out of food, we'll die from starvation, and that's not a good way to go. The pills offer us a peaceful alternative. They'll allow us to go with dignity."

I couldn't believe I was using Cliff Rogers' words!

"I don't want a peaceful alternative!" Sean nearly roared, and I placed my hand on his shoulder to steady him. "I'm not dying, dad! I'm not taking any pills! I'm going to live!"

"Shh," I hushed him. Like father like son. "I'm not taking any pills either. Neither are you or Anthony."

"Promise?"

"I promise."

I wrapped my arms around Sean and hugged him. Feeling his warm body pressed against my own, I allowed myself to feel the presence of my dear, late grandfather. He stood behind me and placed his large hand on my shoulder. I could see him there, with his characteristic smirk, and I could hear him, saying, "You're going to be all right. You and your family."

I had been aware for some time of Anthony's voice. He'd been saying something but I'd been so caught up with my talk with Sean I hadn't answered, and neither had anyone else. It's tough being a four-year-old, very tough getting anyone's attention. He must have been trying for a long time, because all of a sudden he just up and shouted, "I see the sun!"

All of us turned to look at Anthony. He stood pointing at one of the boarded up windows, with Lara by his side.

"I see the sun!" he shouted again.

Through the boarded plank we saw for the first time the faintest whisper of white light.

"I think the kid's right!" Belieau said.

"Glory be to God!" McIntyre cried out.

We ran towards the wall, and Belieau and Rogers immediately grabbed a couple of hammers from the floor and ripped the nails from one of the boards, tearing it away. They looked through the newly created space.

"I see it! It's the sun!" Belieau cried. "The sun's back! Look! Look, everyone!"

He made room, and we scurried forward.

Over the horizon, as if it had never left, the sun was shining.

Within a few hours, the temperature outside had returned to a normal 75 degrees. The trickling of water was everywhere.

There would be massive flood problems, no doubt, but no one cared. The sun was shining again.

Somebody who had a boom box was playing a recording of George Harrison's "Here Comes the Sun," and to this glorious theme, we hugged, rejoiced, cried, and said our good-byes as we slowly made our way back to the above-ground world outside.

It didn't take us long to find our minivan, still parked where we had left it. It was dead, of course, like most of the other vehicles around town, its engine and battery killed by the cold and ice. So we returned home on foot and were there within twenty-minutes.

I had just about opened the front door when a blue Mercury Sable station wagon pulled into the driveway. It was Lara's parents and brothers, and after a tearful reunion with her family, Lara shed tears again as she said goodbye to Sean and Anthony, and to me. They drove away, and suddenly it was oh so quiet.

I opened the front door, and the three of us entered the living room.

"Home sweet home," Anthony said, breaking the eerie silence.

It was extremely stuffy inside. I had closed all the windows when the temperature had plummeted. I began going around the house flinging open all the windows when to my amazement I heard a sound that at first I thought I had only imagined. And then I heard it again.

From the backyard.

A dog's bark.

"No way!" I shouted, as I ran to the back door. Sean and Anthony heard it too, and they were quickly upon my heels.

I opened the back door and a soaked Scout bounded in like insanity on four legs, jumping on us, falling to the floor, barking, jumping on us again. He didn't know what to do with himself he was so happy.

"How the hell did you do it?" I asked, petting him incessantly.

He answered by looking up at me with ecstatic eyes that seemed to say, "I don't know! I'm just happy to be here!"

As Sean and Anthony hugged and kissed Scout, I stepped

onto the back porch to check the backyard. I found the remnants of a tunnel of sorts in the melting snow which led to Scout's dog house. He must have found his way home (a miracle in itself!) and then tunneled through the snow down to his dog house, where he survived for those three days. I assumed he avoided dehydration by eating snow.

I made Scout a huge bowl of Dog Chow and set it on the kitchen floor. He wolfed down the food like a starving puppy.

"You're Scout the Wonder Dog!" I said.

"When is mom coming home?" Anthony asked.

His words punched me in the gut and took my breath away.

The road in front of our home was like a parade on the Fourth of July. Cars were riding up and down the street, horns blasting, American flags waving, people cheering, hooting, waving.

On our front porch were four rocking chairs. With Scout lying by our feet, Sean, Anthony, and I sat on three of them, rocking back and forth gently. The fourth chair remained empty and still.

We watched the cars drive by, watched other people celebrate, as absent family members returned home to the neighborhood, and joyful reunions were made. Everyone seemed to be getting back together.

We watched and waited for our turn.

We looked longingly for Catherine's silver Volvo to roll around the bend and pull into the driveway. Sean and Anthony talked endlessly about running out to the driveway to give their mommy a great big hug.

I wanted to hug her too. As difficult as things had grown between us, hatred really hadn't become an issue. Neither one of us had grown so bitter that we hated the other.

I looked skyward at the sun burning as brightly and as powerful as it always had before.

Speculation was all over the airwaves. What really had happened to the sun? No one knew.

I'm sure that in time the answer will be discovered. My money is on that magnetic anomaly theory Jim McIntyre had talked about.

Yet, there's a part of me that believes the laws of science had very little to do with what happened. I was an English major in college, my concentration being the Romantic poets. I had particularly enjoyed William Blake and was fond of his belief that poets not scientists wrote of reality. Thinking of Blake, I couldn't help but wonder, what if the sun disappeared by choice?

What if it were just sick and tired of looking down upon the Earth and seeing mankind make one bad decision after another? What if it no longer wanted to be part of our world? What if it simply had said, "The hell with it! I've had enough! I quit!"

What if that's what really happened?

"We are sickening," I thought. "If I were a star looking down upon us I might want out too."

But there up in the sky the sun was shining again.

"It came back," I thought. "The separation was only temporary. We have a second chance."

I couldn't help but feel optimistic, even though for all I knew, for all anyone knew, the darkness could come again.

I rose from my chair and hugged both Sean and Anthony, and I heard my grandfather's voice. "You'll be all right."

The three of us continued rocking, Scout by our feet, until sunset, waiting, waiting, with a firm, unwavering confidence that our patience would be rewarded.

This vampire tale was published in 2011 in EPITAPHS, the first anthology published by the New England Horror Writers, and edited by a very talented author and friend, Tracy L. Carbone. I had written "Chuck the Magic Man Says I Can" about ten years earlier, and when it failed to find a home, I put it aside for several years and then worked on a bunch of rewrites and changed the title, and lucky for me, Tracy liked it.

CHUCK THE MAGIC MAN SAYS I CAN

Dee wasn't a violent girl, but jamming a pick-ax into Shirley's head would have suited her just fine.

"I don't want you going into that room, understand?" Aunt Shirley said. "Don't you roll your eyes at me, young lady!"

"I wasn't rolling my eyes," Dee lied. She turned her back on Shirley and gave her the finger.

"Aunt" Shirley wasn't even her real aunt. She and "uncle" Trevor were simply friends of her parents who owned a great big farmhouse in the boonies of New Hampshire. Big deal! Just because they had space enough for two teenage girls, and because Trevor and her dad were such good friends, they got to spend weeks on end at the farmhouse while her mom and dad enjoyed some "honey honey" time (whatever the hell that was-the things her mom said sometimes) in Europe or wherever the hell they wanted to go without their daughters. The bottom line: her parents were out seeing the world and she was stuck with Shirley the Nazi witch from hell.

It wasn't like they weren't old enough to be on their own. She was fourteen, and Fay was seventeen, but her parents preferred that they had adult supervision, or as her mom liked to say, "adult company." Adult company was fine, but did it have to be Shitty Shirley? Trevor was okay. She didn't have any problems with him. He was a real person after all. But Shirley— somewhere in her family tree she had a relative named Satan.

"It's locked so you can't go in there anyway," Aunt Shirley said.

Why she just couldn't drop the subject, Dee didn't know.

"I just want you two girls to know the room is off limits."

"Sure, no problem, Aunt Shirley. We won't go in there," Fay said, forever the peacemaker.

"Thank you, Fay. You're a good girl," Shirley said.

Dee hardened her face until she felt like Humphrey Bogart. She had no use for boring old black and white movies, but recently she had sat down with her dad and taken in CASABLANCA. She had actually liked it. She especially liked Bogart. She liked the way he took orders from no one. He did what he wanted when he wanted, and he didn't let anyone get in his way. He also looked out for himself. He stuck his neck out for nobody, she remembered him saying in the movie.

Bogart would have slapped Shirley across the face hard. Dee wished she could slap her aunt's face. Hard.

"It's your uncle's private place," Shirley said.

Was she still talking about that damn room?

"His refuge from the world," Shirley went on. "Ever since he started working the third shift, he's become protective of his private space. It's less the shift and more his new boss. He really gets to him."

"No," Dee thought. "*You* get to him. How did he ever marry you in the first place? He's so laid back and normal, and you're a beast, the Queen Mother from Hell."

Dee waited until Fay had fallen asleep on the recliner in the living room, her copy of Dostoyevsky's *The Idiot* open and resting on her chest. She didn't know how her sister could fall asleep in the middle of the day, especially here. The farmhouse was as bright as a bomb blast and just as pleasant. There were huge windows everywhere, filling the place with sunshine. You'd think with light like this the place would be cheery and full of happiness, but nope, it was as cold as a coffin, further proof that dear old aunt Shirley was a witch. The bright light combined with the white snow on the ground outside practically blinded Dee and made her eyes water.

Winter vacation, and she was stuck here. She should have been off skiing.

"We'll do the family trip next vacation," her mom had said.

Gee, thanks. Not that she was ungrateful, but she had a life, too, and didn't her opinion count for something? She had told her parents time and time again her feelings about Shirley, but it didn't seem to matter. Here she was again.

The Castle of Death. It was up to her to liven things up.

She stood at the bottom of the stairs. At the top waiting for her was *the room that thou shall not enterest.*

"Well, Aunt Shirley, I'm going to enter it just to piss you off." Dee climbed the stairs.

Smack dab in front of her was *the* room, her uncle's private playroom, or whatever the hell it was.

Funny, Dee hadn't thought before of invading Trevor's privacy. That wouldn't be cool. She was doing it only to spite Shirley. So, she thought, she'd just go inside the room for the sake of saying she did. She wouldn't snoop or look at any private stuff Trevor might have in there. Oh, maybe she would, if it looked interesting. For some reason, she didn't think Trevor would mind.

Dee grabbed the doorknob. It was locked, just like Shirley had said. Lucky for her, this wouldn't be a problem.

Dee reached inside the right pocket of her sweatshirt and pulled out the key she had bought from Chuck the Magic Man.

Chuck the Magic Man, now there's a name she hadn't said lately. She hadn't been into his store to buy anything in months, not since her mom had taken away her allowance, just because she refused to do her homework. Big deal. Parents!

Chuck owned the tiny downtown comics and collectibles shop she liked to visit, "Chuck the Magic Man's Magic Shoppe." It was one of those stores that was about as big as her bathroom yet had enough stuff in it to fill a supermarket. She loved going in there. It smelled like bubble gum and pipe tobacco, cherry pipe tobacco, to be exact.

She liked Chuck. There weren't a whole lot of adults Dee enjoyed being around, but Chuck was one of them. Trevor was another.

Chuck liked her too. He always sold her things real cheap, like the key.

"Opens all locks," he had told her, and it was no lie because Chuck never lied to her. Everything he had told her about his products had been true, like the deck of cards that contained directions for forty tricks, all of them easy to perform with foolproof results. She had never been one for card tricks, but with this deck, she fooled everybody, and it *was* easy.

Chuck would smile at her with his long curly brown hair and chipped front tooth. He wasn't a particularly good looking man, but he always smelled good, like soap and cologne, and he looked clean. He reminded her of that pirate from those movies, Captain Jack Sparrow, only he was older.

But Dee's favorite thing about Chuck was his attitude.

"You can do anything you want," he'd tell her. "As long as you put your mind to it."

And then he'd add," Just study hard and do well in school so you can go off to college and get a good job. Don't be like me, stuck working in a store like this."

"But I'd love to work here!" She'd tell him. "I love this store!"

"Why would you want to work here? Set higher goals for yourself. Remember, *you can do anything you want*."

He said that to her so much, that she found herself saying it at home.

"I can *too* do that! Chuck the Magic Man says I can!"

She truly believed her parents had grown to hate the name, Chuck the Magic Man.

Oh well. Too bad for them!

She inserted the key into the lock and turned it.

Click!

"Thanks, Chuck!" she said silently.

She guided the door open with her left hand, and it opened silently, without even a creak.

She slipped inside the door, closed it again, and locked it, shutting Shirley and the rest of the world out. Dee was safe.

She turned around and saw the coffin.

She momentarily lost her breath and jumped backwards, bumping the door with a thud, which was the last thing she wanted to do.

There was no mistaking that it was a coffin. She had been to her share of funerals. Her parents had lots of old relatives, and more than a few had had their batteries run dry. She knew what a coffin looked like.

The question in her mind right now was, what was it doing here in the middle of her uncle's private room?

Her first thought was that he was a vampire, and she only thought this because of all those damn teenage vampire romance books her friends continually read. What crap! She had read Stephen King's SALEM'S LOT against her mother's wishes (of course!) because her mom said she was too young, but she loved it, just as her sister Fay had said she would. Dee had perused the pages of more than a few of those vampire romances, and they were pure fluff compared to King's book. Anyway, Uncle Trevor a vampire was the most ridiculous thought she had ever had, and she quickly dismissed it.

So, why was there a coffin here? Perhaps this wasn't Uncle Trevor's room at all. Perhaps this room simply housed Aunt Shirley's dirty little secret. That made more sense to Dee. Shirley was keeping a dead body in the house. Whose dead body was it, and why was Shirley keeping it locked away in a bedroom all its own?

She didn't know about the second question, but she knew how to answer the first.

But did she have the guts? Yeah, she did.

She prided herself on the fact that she didn't frighten easily. In fact, she didn't frighten at all. Her dad could bring Fay to tears just with a stern look, a silent expression, but with Dee, his icy stares accomplished nothing. He could shout, rant, stamp his foot, all to no effect. Dee would simply sit there with that hardened expression on her face. It was in her constitution, she guessed, in her blood. She was, in the words of her mom, "one tough cookie."

She chewed the inside of her cheek, a nervous habit she had

yet to shake. Okay, maybe it wasn't going to be as easy as she first thought.

She looked around the room.

There was very little furniture other than the coffin. There was an end table to her right with a lamp on it, and a chair next to the table that looked like a king's chair with its thick fancy legs, as if it belonged in a castle, the Castle of Death.

To her left, she saw an antique dresser of some kind with thin curvy legs that reminded her of the crests of ocean waves. It had tons of tiny drawers, each equipped with a tiny knob. Dee had seen a dresser like this before, in her grandmother's spare room, except her grandmother's had a mirror. This one didn't.

Behind her and to her left was a sliding door which was open just a crack. She peeked inside and saw men's clothes hanging from a rack. It was a closet. It smelled of moth balls.

She covered her nose and realized she was still holding Chuck the Magic Man's key. She shoved it back into her sweatshirt pocket and wrapped her arms around herself. It was cold inside the room, much colder than the rest of the house. She spied a heating vent in the floor. Strangely, it was closed shut.

"Shirley wants the heat off in this room. A dead body roasting in a warm room would probably smell bad," Dee thought to herself. "There's a body in that coffin."

The time had come for her to find out once and for all.

She felt along the edge of the coffin, probing with her fingers for a natural spot to lift. She didn't find any, so she decided to simply grab the lid and lift.

It gave way. She opened it quickly, saw a body, and stopped. She groaned inadvertently, swallowed, chewed the inside of her cheek like a squirrel gnawing on an acorn, and then—she lifted some more, until it was all the way open and she could see clearly the body lying in state in front of her was indeed her Uncle Trevor.

"Oh my God!" she whispered to herself.

She stepped back and covered her face with her hands. She wasn't about to scream, but she wanted to make sure not even a peep escaped her lips.

She rubbed her chin while she thought. It was Uncle Trevor all right, and he was dead. His flesh was a sickening shade of blue, and he wasn't breathing. She suddenly wanted to cry. She loved Uncle Trevor, but she didn't do crying. She simply sniffed instead, as if she had a slight cold coming on.

When she sniffed, she caught a whiff of a slightly putrid odor, like body odor mixed with wet clothing. It wasn't quite as bad as her dad's sweaty socks, but it wasn't pleasant by any means. This smell told her that Trevor had been dead a while, which made no sense to her since she had seen him alive the day before. Did dead bodies stink that quickly?

A wave of anger overcame her. Was this what it was all about? Trevor had died, and Shirley didn't want to tell them? Was it possible that Shirley was this cold-hearted, that she could actually cover up her husband's death like this? Dee easily saw Shirley as the demonic bitch that she was, but this was really out there.

Plus it made no sense. What was Shirley planning to do? Wait the remaining five days of their stay before doing anything?

Dee studied her uncle's face. His eyes were closed tight, as were his lips. His hands were clasped together resting on his belly, as if he were enjoying an afternoon nap. He wasn't wearing any shoes, just socks, which was no surprise since no one wore shoes in Shirley's house.

She looked back at his face. There was a slight gap between his top and bottom eyelashes that hadn't been there before. But how could that be? He was dead.

Yet, as she watched his face, she saw his eyes slowly, slowly open. She clenched the edge of the coffin tightly. His eyes were blank, at first, as if they were blind. Then he blinked—yes, the dead body of her uncle lying in front of her actually blinked— and his pupils turned gradually towards her until he looked directly at her.

It took him a moment, it seemed, to recognize her. Once he did, the blank expression left his face. A look of fear replaced it.

Dee didn't say a word. Neither did Trevor. They remained that way for a short while, motionless, eyes locked, mouths silent.

Something touched Dee's hand. Trevor's hands were still clasped over his belly. She looked down. A large brown cockroach had scurried onto the back of her right hand, and there it had stopped, as if it too were staring into Trevor's eyes.

Dee didn't have a problem with bugs. Fay would scream if she saw a spider, but Dee picked up spiders, roaches, worms, you name it. She even handled bees. They didn't bother her.

She reached over with her left hand and picked up the roach. She wasn't sure why. She held it in between her left index finger and thumb, in front of her face, examining it curiously. She looked back at Trevor. He was examining the bug as well. His lips parted, revealing his teeth. A pair of fangs protruded prominently from his mouth.

"No—way," Dee thought.

She felt the cockroach in between her fingers, struggling to get away. She watched Trevor's face closely. As he continued to eye the roach in between her fingers, drool dripped from his lips.

"Do you want this?" she asked, jiggling her hand, shaking the bug.

Trevor's lips slowly parted into a devilish grin.

Dee extended her hand towards Trevor's face and dangled the roach above his mouth. His eyes widened. She dropped the roach, and it landed on his lips. He snapped at it and sucked it inside his mouth. Keeping his lips closed tightly together, he chewed the bug as if he were eating a crunchy cookie and swallowed.

There was almost a look of embarrassment on his face, as if he were ashamed that Dee had discovered his secret, but Dee's stone cold expression, which showed neither fear nor disgust, seemed to reassure him, and his face relaxed.

"It's okay," she said. "I won't tell."

And she wouldn't. She liked Trevor. Had it been Shirley in the coffin, she would have been pounding that wooden stake into her chest like there was no tomorrow.

Dee lay awake in the hard uncomfortable bed. The accommodations were always the same, ironing board mattresses, sandpaper sheets, starch stiff blankets tucked in tight, and pillows as soft as tires. She didn't sleep much at Shirley's.

The room was dark. The only light came from the window, from the glowing moon hovering in the night sky. Its pale rays cut across the room and fell upon Dee's legs. She lay outside the covers because underneath she felt trapped, pinned in a cocoon spun by Shirley. She hated that feeling. She needed to be free.

The bedroom door was shut, and no light seeped in from the hall beyond it. The old-fashioned clock on the wall ticktocked loudly. It was the only sound she heard until the floor creaked.

Trevor stood by the foot of her bed.

The door hadn't opened. Even though she couldn't see it clearly in the low light, she knew it hadn't opened because it squeaked. She would have heard it. It was the dead of winter. Though the shade was up, the window was closed. How Trevor could have got into the room she had no idea.

She chewed the inside of her cheek. She said nothing.

Trevor stood above her head, towering over her as she lay in bed. He looked her in the eye, and she looked right back. His face seemed full of curiosity, as if he were wondering what it was that made her tick, as if he were trying to understand her lack of emotion.

"It's simple, really," she thought. "I do what I want when I want, and as long as I'm true to myself, there's nothing you can do about it. Chuck the Magic Man says so."

She wondered if Trevor could read minds. She didn't think so, because he still wore the same curious expression on his face. She wasn't going to make it easy for him either. She hit him with her best icy glare.

He raised his right hand and brought it towards Dee's face, as if he were going to stroke her cheek. She noticed he held something in his hand. In between his index finger and thumb, he held a cockroach, its little legs kicking and flailing. Trevor's blue lips parted, and he smiled, exposing his fangs ever so slightly. He looked at the roach and then back at her, as if to say, "You like?"

Dee gritted her teeth and swallowed. She knew what he wanted her to do. She had swallowed a goldfish once. This would be easier. She nodded.

Trevor waited, as if to make sure Dee understood. Then he gently placed the roach on her lips.

It quickly scurried from her mouth up the side of her nose towards her forehead. Just as fast, Dee grabbed the insect, pulling it off her face. Trevor's expression went sour. His face filled with anxiety, as if he feared she were about to ruin the moment, but she didn't toss the bug onto the floor. Instead, she calmly lowered it to just above her lips. She opened her mouth wide and dropped the roach inside.

She closed her mouth and chewed, slowly, methodically, as if she were savoring each and every bite, as if nothing she had ever eaten had tasted this good. The reality was far from it. The roach tasted horribly bitter, like blood mixed with dirt. She tried to make things better by imagining she was eating sunflower seeds. After several seconds, the taste of blood in her mouth became less nauseating, and she didn't have to pretend any longer that she was enjoying the experience. The coppery taste grew on her, as she rolled around the bits and pieces now mixed with her saliva inside her mouth, touching each morsel with her tongue, pausing to play with it against her teeth.

"Mmm," she moaned slowly.

Trevor trembled ever so slightly, and he wiped drool from his lips.

Slowly, she swallowed.

"Mmm," she moaned again. "That was good."

She suddenly felt exposed, as if she were lying naked in front of him.

He smiled at her gently and said, "It's okay. I won't tell."

Shirley scurried this way and that about the house, in a tiff, muttering, "He said this wouldn't happen!"

Dee sat in the living room playing her latest game on her PSP, occasionally looking up and watching Shirley with amusement. Had Trevor dribbled some blood on her precious rug, Dee smirked?

"Your sister's feeling sick today," Shirley said. "You keep that video contraption on low so the noise doesn't disturb her, you hear?"

Sick? That was the first Dee had heard of it.

Dee knocked on the bedroom door. Fay lay in bed, the covers pulled up to her chin.

"Shirley said you're sick?" Dee asked.

Fay nodded and coughed. "I feel awful. I think it's the flu."

Fay did look unbearably pale. Dee touched her sister's forehead. It was icy cold.

"You don't feel feverish," Dee said.

"I don't know about that. I've got the chills," Fay said. She sneezed and turned her head, so that she wouldn't sneeze on her sister.

Dee saw two tiny puncture wounds on her sister's throat.

She retreated to the basement. She wanted to be alone, to think. She looked ahead of her, at Trevor's tool bench, covered with hammers, saws, screwdrivers, and files. Gathering dust in the corner next to the bench sat several flimsy wooden chairs. It would be easy to break them apart, to take one of those wooden chair legs and sharpen it to a point.

She looked down at the floor.

A roach crossed the cement terrain.

There was only one person in the entire world who Dee felt understood her completely, and who she loved unconditionally, and that was her sister, Fay. She meant the world to Dee, and Dee would do anything to protect her.

Dee looked down at the roach on the floor. She stomped on it with her foot, and crushed it, crushed it until it was an unrecognizable blotch of bloody bits and pieces.

Dee stood in front of the coffin.

She placed the hammer and stake she had crafted from the wooden chair leg under her right armpit and squeezed them tight, holding them there, while with both her hands she pushed open the coffin lid. It was heavy at first, but once more it opened rather easily, with that slight creak.

She huffed in frustration.

The coffin was empty.

Did he know? Did Trevor know she was coming after him? Could he read minds? She never remembered any of the vampires she had come across in books and movies possessing the ability to read minds.

She heard a low rumbling sound, and she remembered the closet with the sliding door. She looked up to see Trevor step from the closet. He hadn't read her mind, because he looked surprised to see her.

Dee felt a sudden draft of cold air blowing from the closet, and it smelled musty, like a basement. She bet there was a secret passageway from the closet to the basement. She bet there were other secret passageways too, which would explain how Trevor had gotten in and out of her bedroom without using the door or window.

Trevor pointed to the hammer and stake.

"Why?" he asked.

"You bit my sister," Dee said. "Now you have to pay."

"Would you rather it had been you?" Trevor asked.

"For your sake, it should have been me," Dee said, without missing a beat.

The door to the room burst open, and Shirley turned on a light.

"What's going on, here? Trevor, what are you doing?" she asked, her face full of horror, as if she had caught her husband in bed with another woman.

"Shirley, help me!" Dee said.

"Help *you*? You little bitch! Why on earth would I help you?" Shirley said. She turned to her husband. "Kill her."

Trevor shook his head.

"What do you mean, no?" Shirley said. "You have no choice. You think she's going to keep her mouth shut about you? Think again! With that trap of hers she'll tell the whole world. You have to kill her! *If you don't, I will.*"

Dee couldn't believe what she was hearing. Shirley was a royal bitch, but a murderer? She fought to keep her wits about her. She had to think fast.

"You'll never get away with killing me," Dee said. "Trevor, it makes no sense for me to die. I'm young. But Shirley over there, if she died, no one would suspect a thing. She's old! If you're going to kill anyone, kill her."

"Why you little tramp!" Shirley said. "Trevor won't kill me.

He needs me. I keep him safe. And before you get any ideas, old man, about listening to your little slut here, you just remember who keeps your coffin protected all day. You think she's going to move in here and take care of you? Keep dreaming!"

What Dee said next came out of her mouth so fast she had trouble believing she was saying it. "Maybe I will take care of Trevor. Maybe I'm sick of my parents and want to move away from them. Maybe I want to move in here. Maybe I can satisfy Trevor in ways in which you haven't even thought of, Shirley! You called me a tramp! Well, you're right! I'll do things with Trevor that you don't even know exist! Kill her, Trevor! Kill her! I'm yours if you kill her! Feel my body in your arms right now!"

She ran to him, and he wrapped his arms around her.

"I feel good, don't I, Trevor?" Dee said. "Kill her, Trevor, and I'm yours! Do it!"

"Don't be stupid, Trevor," Shirley said, trying to sound confident. But she didn't sound confident. She sounded scared.

"Feel me," Dee said. "Kill her."

Trevor let go of Dee, and she no sooner had taken a deep breath when she was suddenly witnessing the unthinkable: Trevor grabbing Shirley by the neck and ripping her head from her shoulders.

Dee screamed.

And then she pulled herself together.

"Trevor, get me a mop!"

For the next hour Dee operated on pure adrenaline, cleaning the floor, wrapping Shirley's headless body and her head in a plastic tarp Trevor had retrieved from his basement work area. And when it was over, when the wood floor had been scrubbed so that only a hint of red remained, she took Trevor by the hand and promised him she'd take good care of him.

"I promise I'll take good care of you, Uncle Trevor. The best care ever! I'll tell my parents I want to stay here for the rest of the school year, that I want to enroll in that private school down the road you and my dad are always talking about. That'll keep me here for the next four years, and after that, we'll figure something out. You just rest now. I'll take good care of you."

Trevor reached for her shirt. She brushed his hand away.

"Not now. I'm too upset. Tomorrow. I promise," she said. "I'll be worth the wait, believe me. I'm going to take such good care of you, such really good care."

Dee opened the coffin and watched as the bright sunlight from the large window bore down upon Trevor's sleeping body. It smoked at first and then sizzled and caught fire. Trevor opened his eyes but didn't seem to see her. He looked at his own body ablaze, and screamed in terror for about ten seconds before the flames consumed him.

When he had been reduced to ash, Dee slammed the lid shut.

Dee pressed speed dial on her cell phone.

"Hello, mom? It's Dee. Mom, don't panic or be upset, but I have bad news to tell you. Fay and I are fine. It's not us. What? Yes, Fay was sick, but she's better now. I helped her get better. But listen, mom, it's not us. It's Aunt Shirley and Uncle Trevor. Something horrible has happened. Something truly horrible. I don't even know if I can tell you."

Dee felt Chuck the Magic Man's key in her pocket. She squeezed it tight.

"There was a fire—"

She listened as her mother spoke to her in soothing tones, asking for more information, before requesting that she speak with Fay. As Dee handed the phone to her older sister, she thought again about her chances of getting away with this. She had had her doubts, but now, as she squeezed that key tight, she heard Chuck the Magic Man's voice, even felt his breath on her skin.

"Did you put your mind to it?" she heard him ask.

"Yes."

"Then you can do it," Chuck said.

And she knew then she could.

The final story in this collection, "Innocence Undead" was written in honor of Peter Cushing, the actor whose performances in the movies inspired me to become a horror writer. This story features Van Helsing from DRACULA, and it's written with Peter Cushing's interpretation of the character in mind. It was published in 2004 on the Peter Cushing web site http://www.petercushingmuseum.com/innocenceundead.htm.

INNOCENCE UNDEAD

For Peter Cushing

"—A simple child,
That lightly draws its breath,
And feels its life in every limb,
What should it know of death?"

—William Wordsworth *We Are Seven* (1798)

"Tell me about the child," Van Helsing said.

The vampire hunter stood face to face with the man who had invited him to Karlsbruck, Father Butler, inside Butler's modest rectory, with fresh rolls and a bottle of red wine on a small table behind them. Van Helsing had declined both, deciding he wanted to discuss business first. He hadn't even removed his overcoat.

"It started about three years ago," the priest said. He poured himself a glass of wine and did all he could not to spill it. His hands trembled as he brought the glass to his lips and drank.

"The boy fell ill with a disease. The doctors could not cure him. They couldn't even agree as to what he had. The one thing they did agree on was that he was dying. The boy's parents, the Baron and Baroness Tarken, panicked. They evicted the doctors from the castle and began searching for other innovative and unorthodox methods of treatment. They opened their doors to midwives, witch doctors, even Satanists, all in a desperate attempt to save their son. But despite their best efforts, nothing changed. The boy only grew worse."

"What happened?" Van Helsing asked.

"We were visited by the devil, is what happened, Dr. Van Helsing," Father Butler said, his brow moist with perspiration. "Convinced her son was going to die, the Baroness took some bed sheets and hung herself. Her husband, the Baron, found her. She had left a note. She wrote that she couldn't see her son suffer any longer. She knew he was going to die, and she wanted to be there in the next life ahead of him, so she could take care of him."

Van Helsing thought of his own wife and son, young Abraham, about the same age as the Tarken boy. For a moment he shared the pain of Baron Tarken and understood such pain doesn't leave a man whole.

"Hours after the Baroness' funeral, a man came to the castle," Butler continued. "According to the villagers, this man was a vampire. He took the child and with his kiss turned him into an undead, thus in the Baron's eyes, saving his life. Did this really happen? I don't know. However, the boy was suddenly, miraculously 'cured.' That was three years ago. Since that time, villagers, mostly young children, have disappeared in the night. Some abducted from their own bedrooms. They say it is the young Tarken child, that he is a vampire feasting on other children."

"What do you say?" Van Helsing asked.

"I'm no expert. I couldn't tell a vampire from a vegetarian. But this much I do know. Children are disappearing. There have been reports—" Butler paused, he was choked up. He cleared his throat. "There have been reports that some of these missing children have reappeared in the middle of the night, at the windows of their homes, only to disappear again after attacking their parents. And the young Tarken child is no longer seen in the daytime, and when he is seen, they say he hasn't changed one bit, that he still looks seven even though he should be ten. I have seen him myself, and while yes he still looks young, how much of a difference is there between a seven-year-old and a ten-year-old? We definitely have a problem here in Karlsbruck, but whether it is vampirism or not, well, that's why I've asked you here, doctor."

"What would you like me to do?" Van Helsing asked.

Father Butler cleared his throat again. "I want you to examine the boy, to determine whether he's a vampire or not, and if he is—God forgive me, I want you to destroy him."

The Castle Tarken stood majestically on the mountainside, overlooking the tiny village of Karlsbruck like a proud father at his son. It was not the largest castle Van Helsing had ever seen, nor the most elaborate, but it served its purpose. It let the villagers know that within the stone walls of the castle lived a separate class of people, a superior class.

Van Helsing and Father Butler rode in the doctor's tiny black buggy, pulled by a single white horse, until they reached the castle gate. The rest of the trip they had to make on foot, along a dirt path up a steep incline.

It was a beautiful morning full of bright sunshine and fresh air. Birds were singing everywhere.

They reached the castle door, and Van Helsing noticed that the birds had stopped singing. He had experienced this phenomenon before. The presence of evil made even the smallest of creatures uncomfortable.

Up close, the castle looked run-down. Large cracks had begun to appear in the outer stone walls, and the greenery around the grounds was unkempt and wild.

The servant who greeted them at the door refused to let them in. Van Helsing and Butler had expected as much. Baron Tarken kept to himself and rarely allowed visitors. When they had made it clear to the servant that they weren't going away, at least not until they had spoken to Baron Tarken himself,

Van Helsing and Butler breathed a sigh of relief as the servant finally conceded and left them by the door while he summoned his master.

Baron Tarken ignored his servant's meager attempt to apologize and in a manner that suggested he was quite irritated, marched towards the entrance, apparently, to berate Van Helsing and Father Butler for the disturbance.

The Baron was a tall thin man, several inches taller than Van Helsing, and his face was all angles. He had a diamond-shaped head, with slanted eyes, an angular nose that looked to be as sharp as an ice pick, a tight mouth, and a triangular chin that came to a point like a church spire.

His flesh was pale, his eyes dark, with deep purple circles all around, and his lips were unnaturally red. His straight hair was slicked back and was prematurely gray in many places, especially around the edges. He looked like a man who had suffered greatly, as Van Helsing knew he had.

"Father Butler, what do I owe this—visit?" the Baron "greeted," though it was painfully clear he was only interested in ridding himself of the two men.

Father Butler introduced Van Helsing as "Dr. Abrams," a disease specialist who had been called in to treat a new virus that was affecting the area's children. Butler and Van Helsing had agreed upon the use of an alias because Van Helsing's reputation as a vampire hunter was renowned all across Europe, even though he'd been "retired" for nearly a decade. Yet few people knew what he looked like.

Father Butler was still explaining the reason for their visit when the Baron interrupted him.

"That's all very good, Father, but I assure you, my son does not have this disease."

"It's highly contagious and easily passable," Van Helsing said.

The Baron shook his head. "My son does not socialize with other children, and he certainly spends no time in the village where you say this disease is ravaging. I'm disappointed in you, Father. I would have expected you to know this in advance."

Father Butler stammered for words. Van Helsing spoke first.

"It's not passed from child to child," Van Helsing said. "But from animal to child. Horses, goats, sheep, they're the carriers. Does your son not have contact with such animals?"

The Baron paused, his mouth wide open. Van Helsing's revelation had obviously come as a surprise to him.

"What's the name of this disease?" the Baron asked.

Van Helsing made up the most confusing Latin name he could think of.

The Baron nodded. "I see. Why haven't I heard of it before?"

"It has reached this area only recently," Van Helsing said. "We've traced its origins to southeast Asia, but it is spreading throughout Europe like wildfire."

"It's fatal, you say?" The Baron asked.

Van Helsing nodded.

"Well, I suppose you should see him, then. Let me see if he is awake. My servant Lawrence will send for you presently."

The Baron took leave of them.

Father Butler tugged softly on Van Helsing's sleeve and whispered, "From what you've told me, if the boy were truly a vampire, he'd be unable to succumb to disease, and the Baron would know this. He must not be a vampire, then."

"Not necessarily," Van Helsing answered quietly. "A father's love runs deep. I know. Even if he believes with absolute certainty that his son cannot die, once the possibility of death is suggested, he may out of fear and natural parental worry begin to doubt his own convictions. Besides, you've described the Baron as a very shrewd individual. It would be somewhat suspicious if he rejected our help outright, and I don't think that's the kind of attention the Baron wants."

Lawrence the servant returned to the castle entrance and ushered Van Helsing and Father Butler up an elegant set of stairs to the castle's second level.

They walked a very dark corridor. Van Helsing noticed that all the blinds and curtains on the windows had been drawn.

The Baron stood at the end of the long hallway, waiting outside an opened door.

"This way, gentlemen," the Baron said. He motioned with his hand for the two men to enter the room. "This way."

Van Helsing moved first.

The Baron grabbed the doctor by his right arm.

"You're here strictly to examine, not medicate, correct?" the Baron asked.

Van Helsing nodded.

"Good. You may see Justin now," the Baron said.

Van Helsing entered the room, with Father Butler and the Baron right behind him.

Young Justin's room was even darker than the rest of the castle. The large window behind the bed was completely covered with a pair of massive wooden shutters. Despite of the open books and puzzles strewn about the floor, there was nothing cheery about this room. It was also cold. It reminded Van Helsing of a sepulcher.

The boy, Justin, lay on his back on his bed. Van Helsing approached him and sat on the edge of the bed by the boy's feet.

"Hello, Justin," Van Helsing said. "I am Dr. Abrams. Has your father explained why I'm here?"

"Yes," the boy answered. He yawned.

"I kept him up too late last night, I'm afraid," the Baron said. "Sometimes we get so deep into reading we can't put the book down."

Van Helsing flashed a half smile and began the examination. He touched the boy's wrist to take a pulse, and as he expected it would be, the boy's flesh was ice cold.

"Very good," Van Helsing said.

Justin's flesh was also extremely pale. He looked ill.

Van Helsing continued the examination and finished by checking the boy's mouth.

"You need to check his teeth, too?" the Baron asked.

"Yes," Van Helsing answered, eyeing the pair of sharp fangs inside Justin's mouth. "Thank you, Justin. That'll be all for now."

"Well? What's the verdict?" the Baron asked, as Van Helsing stood from the bed.

"He does not have the disease," Van Helsing said.

The Baron smiled. "Excellent news!"

"However, he should be vaccinated," Van Helsing said. "I can return later in the week with the vaccination."

"I'm sorry, doctor, but I don't believe in vaccines. Or medications for that matter. I try to keep my son's blood as pure as possible," the Baron said.

"I'm sorry to hear that. The vaccine is the one true way to protect your son," Van Helsing said.

"We'll take our chances. He enjoys excellent health. You just examined him, doctor, wouldn't you agree?" the Baron asked.

Van Helsing looked at Justin, then ushered the Baron towards the door. He spoke softly when he said, "I cannot attest to his general health since I was looking for specific symptoms. However, he does seem rather pale and weak. Has he been ill recently?"

"No. He just doesn't like the outdoors. He's a thinker, not a doer."

"I see. Even the thinkers need sunshine," Van Helsing said.

"I'll remember that." The Baron's face hardened. "Good day gentlemen."

"Good day," Van Helsing answered.

Father Butler gulped the wine from the goblet and wished for more.

"How I didn't want this to be true!" he said. "What are we going to do? You speak of driving stakes through hearts. He's a child, for heaven's sake!"

"No," Van Helsing answered firmly. "The child is dead. Justin is now an undead."

"Undead, vampire, all words! It's horrible!" Butler cried.

"It's more than just words, father. Vampirism is a disease that must be stamped out. I don't relish the idea of driving a stake through a young boy's heart, believe me, but if we don't destroy him, your village in fact the entire countryside will be infested with these creatures. We have to destroy him."

The priest paced up and down his rectory. "I don't feel good about this! What are you going to do? Even if you're able to get back into the castle, how would you ever get out?"

"I'm not going back inside the castle," Van Helsing said.

"You're not? What are you going to do, then?"

"Not me. You."

"Me?"

"Sit down, father, and listen. This is what we're going to do."

As Father Butler listened, Van Helsing explained what he had in mind. Father Butler was to instruct his congregation on how to protect themselves from vampires. He was to go door to door to each and every house with the following information. All children were to be kept inside after nightfall. Even during the daylight hours, the children must not be left alone. Crucifixes should be placed above the child's bed. The windows, even on warm nights, had to be locked. Garlic should be placed along the windows and doors. It was imperative, Van Helsing explained, that everyone with children follow these instructions.

"Will they cooperate?" Van Helsing asked.

"Yes, I think so. I don't see why they wouldn't," Father Butler answered. "But what does this achieve?"

"We're going to draw him out, Father," Van Helsing said. "I meant it when I said I wouldn't need to go back to the castle. The boy shall come to us."

Three nights passed without incident. Then, on the fourth evening of the villagers implementing Father Butler's instructions, the most horrid wails exploded from within the castle walls. Young Justin Tarken. Screaming with gut wrenching hunger pains.

"We've cut him off," Van Helsing told Butler in confidence. "Now we shall bait him."

Father Butler had made an arrangement with one of his most faithful parishioner families, the Carlsons. The Carslon family, who had a six-year-old son named Peter, were to leave their son's bedroom exposed. No garlic, no crucifixes, no form of protection whatsoever. Van Helsing and Butler were to be hiding in the adjoining room, awaiting the arrival of the young vampire.

Very few families would have agreed to this arrangement, but the Carlson's had full faith in God, and they said yes to Father Butler's request without hesitation.

One, then two, then three nights passed without any sign of Justin Tarken. Van Helsing admitted he was surprised. When a week had gone by and still there had been no visit by the Tarken boy, Van Helsing was about to rethink his plan when word arrived in Karlsbruck that the child abductions had not ceased after all, but had only moved on to the surrounding villages.

While Van Helsing and Butler sat tight in the Carlson home, two other young children had been abducted from the two villages that boarded Karlsbruck.

In a fit of rage, Van Helsing swore that "not another child" would be harmed by young Justin Tarken. The doctor secluded himself in the back room of Father Butler's rectory, and when he emerged several hours later, he surprised Butler with a request.

"There's something I need to discuss with you," Van Helsing said.

"What is it?" Butler asked.

Van Helsing told him.

"You shouldn't have done that. It's sacrilegious," Butler said.

"I know."

"It might not even work," Butler said.

"I know."

"You could be condemned."

"Father, I know all that, but—"

"It was a damn foolish thing to do!" Butler interrupted. "But—in a way, I'm glad you did it. God knows we need all the help we can get!"

"Pray for me?"

"Of course I will! God be with you, and may He forgive us both!"

The Tarken coach had disappeared.

Van Helsing tugged the reigns and gently stopped the white horse which pulled his buggy.

He listened. He was surrounded by an eerie silence. The moon lit up the night sky above creating shadows all around him. Both sides of the road were heavily wooded, and all he could see were trees and more trees. Of the coach there was no sign.

Yet he knew the coach couldn't be far. He had seen it just a few short moments ago.

He ushered his horse and buggy to the side of the dirt road, jumped to the ground, and walked along the pebbly path. He reached the edge of a hill, below which he saw open fields and the town of Oakwood. The coach was nowhere in sight. It was either behind him somewhere in the woods or down there in front of him, somewhere in Oakwood. Van Helsing didn't know which.

His gut told him that the Tarken coach wouldn't be bold enough to drive directly into the center of town. They'd keep to the shadows, he thought.

Van Helsing turned around.

"They're in the woods," he said to himself.

He started to walk back towards his buggy when he heard the voice of a child. It sounded like a young boy, and he was singing, some sort of nursery rhyme. Van Helsing stopped and listened. The boy was in the woods.

For a brief moment Van Helsing wondered what a child was doing in the woods in the middle of the night, but then he realized the child was there because he had been *called*.

Young Justin Tarken was in the woods too, somewhere, calling to the boy. Van Helsing couldn't hear Tarken, but he was sure of this fact just the same.

Van Helsing broke into a quick trot, running along the road, looking into the woods for any sign of the boy. He had almost made it to his horse and buggy when to his left deep inside the woods he saw the white nightclothes of a young child. The child was skipping, heading in the opposite direction from Oakwood. He was being drawn further away.

Van Helsing entered the woods running and quickly closed the gap between himself and the child.

The boy stopped skipping. With his arms by his side, he appeared to be looking for someone. Van Helsing stopped behind a tree and peered out from behind it.

"I'm here, master," the boy said. "I'm here."

Van Helsing eyed the surroundings. Again there was no sign of Justin Tarken.

"Yes, master, I will do it for you," the boy said. He lifted his little right hand and in it he held a knife, its jagged edge pointed at his own throat.

Van Helsing's eyes widened.

"*No!*" Van Helsing shouted. He charged out from behind the tree and ran towards the boy, and when he reached him, he grabbed his arm and yanked the knife from his hand.

The boy was Justin Tarken.

"Got you!" Justin snarled, rearing back his teeth and showing his fangs.

Van Helsing reached inside his coat and removed a crucifix. He extended it towards the vampire child. Justin hissed and cowered before Van Helsing.

Lawrence the servant appeared behind Van Helsing and struck the doctor in the back of the head with a heavy mallet.

Van Helsing groaned and crumpled to the ground, unconscious.

"Looking for this?"

That's the question Van Helsing heard as he opened his eyes. His head throbbed. He was tied to a table, with tight restraints around his wrists and ankles.

Baron Tarken stood over him. He held Van Helsing's medical bag.

"I didn't think a hammer and stake were standard medical issue these days," the Baron said. "Not to mention a crucifix and a vial of holy water. Only one doctor I know of carries these items, Van Helsing."

"I don't know—"

"Don't deny it," the Baron interrupted. "I've had you followed since you first visited my home. My spies have heard your conversations with the good Father Butler. I know all about you, and what you had in store for my son."

"What are you going to do?" Van Helsing asked.

"What any good father would do. I'm going to protect my son."

"Your son is dead."

"Shut up."

There was a knock at the door, and the servant Lawrence entered the room.

"Get rid of these things. Burn them," the Baron instructed.

"Yes, sir," Lawrence answered. He took Van Helsing's coat and grabbed the crucifix and the medical bag. "I'll be back for the rest in a moment."

Van Helsing wondered what the "rest" was. He looked around the room. It was dark. There was an oil lamp on a table against the wall, providing the only light. He also saw a couple of chairs and a chest. On the chest, in the dim light, he saw the hammer and stake.

"If I thought you'd leave us alone, I wouldn't have to do any of this," the Baron said. "But your reputation precedes you. You never quit. You never stop. Do you? Which leaves me no choice."

"You're going to kill me?" Van Helsing asked.

"I could, and considering who I am, I'd probably get away with it," the Baron answered. "But still, you are known across the continent, and your death or disappearance would certainly cry out for an investigation. I'm too private a person for that. I have better plans for you, and I'm sure you know exactly what they are."

The Baron turned his head. "Come in, Justin."

Young Justin Tarken entered the room and stood by his father.

"What better fate for you, Van Helsing, than to be turned into the very creature you abhor, the creature you have spent your life fighting?" Baron Tarken said. "And what better champion to defeat you than my own son? And the absolute beauty of this plan is that you do not die, you do not disappear. You simply leave.

"I understand you're married with a son of your own," the Baron continued. "You might think me an evil man, but I'm not. I wish your family no harm. If you wish it, I can arrange for them to move to a place where you will not be able to find them, where you will not be able to harm them. What I do now I do to protect my son, and for no other reason."

"Your son is dead," Van Helsing said. "If you truly loved him, you'd untie me and let me—"

"*Don't you ever question my love for my son! How dare you!*" the Baron shouted. "I offer to save your family from you and you insult me? If it were your son, would you do it? Would you drive a shaft of wood through his heart? Would you? *Would you?*"

Van Helsing didn't answer.

"I'll take that as a no," the Baron said. "Now, I'll ask you again. Would you like me to relocate your family? This is the last chance you'll have to tell me."

Van Helsing looked directly into the eyes of Baron Tarken.

"They will do well without your help, thank you," Van Helsing said.

"The words of a proud man," Tarken said. "Unfortunately, sometimes pride gets in the way of common sense. So be it."

The Baron turned to his son. "Justin, he's yours."

The boy stepped towards Van Helsing. Saliva dripped from his open mouth.

Van Helsing took a deep breath. He knew he only had one chance, and it was a chance he wasn't even sure would work. He allowed himself to feel the total anxiety of the moment. As the boy vampire stood above him, Van Helsing began to sweat profusely.

Van Helsing thought of his wife and son, and prayed that he'd be able to see them again. He struggled against the binds, but it was useless. He could see the hammer and stake on the chest, so close but in no way reachable.

The boy placed his small hands upon Van Helsing's shoulder. He opened his mouth wider and closed in towards Van Helsing's sweaty throat.

The Baron looked on expectantly, waiting to hear Van Helsing scream in pain. He was shocked when it was Justin who screamed.

"What is it?" the Baron cried out.

Justin stumbled backwards away from Van Helsing, and he clutched his mouth as if he'd been struck in the face.

"Help me, father!" the boy screamed.

"What is it?" the Baron asked again. He ran to his son. The boy was still covering his mouth. "Are your hurt?" The boy nodded. "Let me see."

The Baron tore the screaming child's hands away from his mouth, and his eyes widened at what he saw. Justin's lips were smoldering, and the flesh around his mouth was bleeding, as if he'd been scalded by boiling water.

The Baron dove towards Van Helsing. *"What did you do to him?"*

Van Helsing didn't answer.

The Baron looked closely at Van Helsing's throat. He saw blood, but it wasn't the doctor's blood. There weren't any wounds on his flesh. His son hadn't broken the doctor's skin. It was his son's blood, intermingled with drops of Van Helsing's perspiration.

"Tell me what you did to him!"

"I drank—holy water," Van Helsing said.

"You drank—" The Baron put two and two together. "It's in your sweat! You bastard! I'll kill you for this!"

The Baron looked wildly around the room. He spotted the hammer and stake and grabbed them both. He waved them in front of Van Helsing's face. "How about this for poetic justice?"

"If you kill me, you won't get away with it," Van Helsing said. "You'll be of no use to your son behind bars."

Justin shrieked, "Father! Help me!"

The Baron looked over his shoulder. "Not now." He placed the point of the wooden stake onto Van Helsing's chest and raised the hammer high above his head.

"Yes, now!" Justin cried. He screamed in agony. "It hurts! *PLEASE!*"

Van Helsing thought quickly. "I can save the boy."

"What?" the Baron asked.

"Untie me, and I'll save him," Van Helsing said.

"Never! You'll kill him!"

"Untie him father!" Justin screamed. "Please!

Justin dropped to the floor, flailing his arms and kicking his legs.

The Baron couldn't help but look at son. The boy's mouth seemed to be melting away. The thought of his child deformed enraged him. He swore, threw the hammer and stake to the floor, and tore from the room. A moment later, he was back with a revolver in his hand. He pointed it at Van Helsing's face.

"If you don't save him immediately, I'll shoot you," the Baron warned.

He attempted to untie Van Helsing, but he couldn't manage with one hand. Against his better judgement, he placed the revolver down upon the chest, and with his two free hands began to untie the doctor.

"I'll need my bag," Van Helsing said.

"No!"

"I can't help him without my bag!"

The Baron growled. He untied Van Helsing's hands and instructed him to untie his own legs. He retrieved the revolver and again aimed it at Van Helsing.

"Justin," the Baron said. "Go and get Lawrence. Tell him to bring the doctor's bag."

"I can't!" the boy cried.

"Do it!"

"Father, I can't!"

"He's in no condition to move," Van Helsing said, having untied his own legs. He stepped from the table and planted his feet firmly upon the floor. "I'll get the bag."

The Baron inserted himself in between Van Helsing and the exit. "No you won't!"

"You'll have to get it then," Van Helsing said.

"And leave you here alone with my son? Do you think I'm crazy?"

"What choice do you have?"

"Lawrence will be back any moment now. I'll send him for the bag."

"There's no time! Look at your son, Baron! Every second you waste—I give you my word as a father, I won't harm your son," Van Helsing said.

"I don't believe you!"

"You're running out of time!" Van Helsing warned. "If you want me to save him, you'll have to act now. Do it, man!"

The Baron moaned. "Your word as a father?"

"Yes! Now go!"

The Baron turned and ran from the room.

Van Helsing looked down upon the floor at the screaming boy. Also on the floor were the hammer and stake, which in his panic, the Baron had forgotten to take with him. Van Helsing crouched down and grabbed the weapons.

He didn't hesitate.

He thrust the boy on his back and pressed the wooden stake upon his chest. Young Justin's eyes widened in terror.

"What are you doing?" Justin cried. "You promised my father!"

"I promised I wouldn't harm his son. You're not his son. Justin Tarken is dead."

"No! I am Justin Tarken! I'm just a little kid! You can't do this to me!"

Van Helsing saw his own son in the boy vampire's eyes. He summoned every ounce of strength within him to block out the cries of this young undead who looked so innocent. Van Helsing focused on the bloody chunks of flesh hanging from the boy's chin and told himself to remember that no ordinary living child would have been so affected by something as harmless as holy water.

"Justin Tarken is dead," Van Helsing said aloud. He raised the hammer.

The boy squealed.

Van Helsing closed his eyes and thrust the hammer down.

Father Butler placed his hands upon Van Helsing's forehead and blessed him.

"You've rid this village of a terrible evil. I know it wasn't easy for you."

"No, it wasn't," Van Helsing whispered.

"Just remember that the child was evil."

"I keep telling myself that."

Butler read the horror on Van Helsing's face, and suddenly experienced doubt. "He was a vampire, wasn't he?"

"Yes."

"Then you did the right thing. Didn't you?"

Van Helsing nodded.

"Still, you're in pain?" Butler asked.

"He was a boy, Father, and this job belongs to men without boys of their own. I'll never shed blood again."

"You'd best be going now," Father Butler said. "The Baron is sure to be on his way. It isn't safe for you to be here."

"What about you?" Van Helsing asked.

"The Baron's not stupid. He won't harm a priest. Be on your guard, Van Helsing. The Baron's reach is far and wide. Protect your family, especially your son."

"Yes, Father, I will."

"God be with you."

Van Helsing climbed into his buggy and tapped the reigns. The white horse broke into a trot and raced along the road into the surrounding countryside, whisking Van Helsing away from the village of Karlsbruck, from the Castle Tarken, and from the horrifying images and memories it contained, memories Van Helsing feared would haunt him for the rest of his days.

So that's it. Those are my stories.

I hope you enjoyed this collection. I know I enjoyed writing them, and I hope to write many more.

Thanks for reading!

—Michael
July, 2018

ABOUT THE AUTHOR

Michael Arruda is the author of the novel *Time Frame*, the short story collections *Dark Corners* and *For The Love of Horror*, and the movie review collection *In The Spooklight*.

He also co-writes the humorous movie review column *Cinema Knife Fight* with fellow author and movie critic L.L. Soares. His *In The Spooklight* horror movie columns can be read each month in The Official Newsletter of the Horror Writers Association. He has published over twenty-five short stories in various markets. You can also read his movie reviews and articles on his blog, This Is My Creation: The Blog of Michael Arruda at marruda3.wordpress.com.

Curious about other Crossroad Press books?
Stop by our site:
http://store.crossroadpress.com
We offer quality writing
in digital, audio, and print formats.

Enter the code FIRSTBOOK
to get 20% off your first order from our store!
Stop by today!